Far Above Rubies

Far Above Rubies

Cynthia Polansky

Martin and Lawrence Press
Groton Massachusetts
2007

Far Above Rubies

Published by
Martin and Lawrence Press
www.martinandlawrencepress.com

ISBN-13: 9780977389827

February 2007

Printed in Canada

This is a work of fiction. Names, characters, and incidents are either the product of the author's imagination or are fictitious. Any resemblance to actual persons or events, living or dead, business establishments, events, or locales are entirely coincidental.

Cover and book design
by Gwyn Snider

For Mieneke,
With love and thanks.

AUTHOR'S NOTE

I first heard Sofie's story at the touring photographic exhibit, *"Anne Frank in the World."* The exhibit culminated in a brief lecture by a Holocaust survivor or second-generation survivor. One particular day, a second-generation survivor spellbound us with vignettes of the Holocaust as told by her aunt Sofie, who had survived Auschwitz. She called her "Tante Soof."

Tante Soof made a deep impression on me. I felt that her story needed to be told to an audience of greater scope than exhibit-goers. What began as a short story evolved into a complex journey delving into the heart and mind of this woman named Sofie. While the basic events that transpire in this novel are factual, I have exercised some literary license with the narrative. Save for historical figures, most names are fictitious, as are some characters. With very few exceptions, however, descriptions of Nazi atrocities are neither exaggerated nor illusory. Though not all may have been inflicted on the real Tante Soof or her family, they did indeed happen to some Holocaust victims somewhere.

Every survivor's story is one of victory, a unique tale that bears telling. Tante Soof is one such victory.

"A woman of valor who can find? for her price is far above rubies."

— PROVERBS

PROLOGUE

Yiskadal, v'yiskadash shimei rabbah ...
The rabbi intoned the eternal words of the mourner's *Kaddish* as the plain pine coffin with the single Star of David carved into the wood was lowered into the ground. I had always felt that reciting *Kaddish* — the Jewish prayer affirming life — was a healthy, positive way to honor the deceased, but never had it seemed more appropriate than now, at Tante Soof's funeral. What better way to say goodbye to a woman who had lived the way I believe God intended. Tante Soof believed that no matter how dark the misfortune, how bleak the prospects, there is always hope. No one can take that away from you. And where there is hope, there is life.

Tante Soof had taught me a great deal. Not only the value of optimism and tenacity in life, but truth. She had told me the truth about what happened during World War II: to her, to my parents, to the innumerable Jews in Europe. I remember Tante Soof telling it all...

I was born on January 6, 1945 in Maarssen, a little town about 18 kilometers south of Amsterdam, on the River Vecht. Mammie had insisted that I be born at home instead of in the small hospital where Pappie was a staff physician. She said she wanted her baby born where the ravages of war could not touch what was really important. We lived in a grand old house that had been built in the seventeenth century. Mammie and Pappie had christened it *"Vredehoop"* — "Hope for Peace."

The winter of 1945 became known as the great Hunger Winter of World War II. Two hundred twenty thousand people in Holland alone died of starvation. The Germans had taken everything to feed themselves, leaving a chronic food shortage in the bigger cities toward the end of 1944. By the winter of '45, the shortage had increased to unbearable proportions that stretched their limits to the whole of Holland. The particularly harsh weather that winter served to exacerbate the circumstances, sapping the Dutch of what little strength they had remaining. Tante Soof used to say that it wasn't enough that we were starving; we had to freeze, too. It was as if we were characters in a Norse myth, she fancied, and the trickster god Loki was having his fun with us. Her ability to find humor in such a wretched state of affairs amazed me.

Desperation drove the people of Maarssen out on "hunger expeditions," seeking out farmers who they prayed had not yet been overrun by the starving townsfolk in a desperate attempt to secure what meager food might still be available. Mammie dug up tulip bulbs and boiled them for the family's supper. The starving often dropped dead in the streets, their wasted bodies unable to survive the cold and wet. For the first five months of my life my only sustenance was sugarwater and what little milk my brothers Wim and Herman could scavenge. Nobody expected me to live, but somehow I survived. Perhaps it was that same stubborn determination that would see me through the trials I was to endure later in life. Perhaps it was merely having been born under the veil of hope.

Naturally, I have no memory of those hard times. As I grew up, Mammie and Pappie were reluctant to relive the hungry days and never discussed them, despite my many questions over the years. The only indication of my parents' ordeal came when I complained of being hungry, as a child often will do.

"Hungry?" my mother chided, "You don't know what hungry is!"

Her response confused me, resulting in an inexplicable feeling of guilt for articulating an innocent and natural sensation. It was only when I reached adulthood that I understood the origins of her criticism.

Still, had it not been for my aunt Sofie's visits to my childhood home, I might never have known the kind of personal struggle for survival my parents and fellow Jews endured during the war

Mammie's younger sister Sofie — whom my brothers and I called "Tante Soof" — was a warm and affectionate woman, full of laughter and love. She filled a room with her presence, as much from her rotund shape as from her zest for living. We always looked forward to Tante Soof's visits.

Wiping her hands on her apron, Mammie looked out the window to see Tante Soof's car pulling into the driveway.

"Children! Tante Soof is here!" she called upstairs.

Never did we have to be coaxed into making an appearance, as many of my school chums did when their relatives visited. I always felt a bit sorry for my shy friend Janni, whose tiresome aunt and uncle always insisted that Janni sing for them during their visits.

Herman, Wim and I raced one another down the stairs, each eager to be the first to be welcomed into Tante Soof's ample embrace. Her dark brown hair, always neatly arranged in soft waves, framed a round, smooth face with smiling red lips and laugh crinkles at the corners of her hazel eyes. Tante Soof had beautiful eyes, but her heavy dark brows dominated her face and diverted one's attention from the grey-green orbs that changed color like a chameleon. Her fair complexion had the look of porcelain, the result of nightly oatmeal facials.

Where her coat parted open, I caught a glimpse of the sunny, cheerful pattern of her dress. Her wardrobe contained an assortment of brightly colored dresses with prints of big, splashy flowers. Tante Soof always said that she had seen too much drabness in this life to ever wear anything but the boldest colors. Little matter that the loud prints did nothing but emphasize her girth. The rather shapeless flowery dresses always put me in mind of an entire garden that had uprooted itself and was marching into our house. I never failed to giggle at the thought.

"*Nu?*" she said, beaming at my brothers and me, "How have you been, my children?" From the enormous pockets of her red cloth coat she pulled out little bags of chocolate caramels, one for each of us.

"Come," Mammie urged, as we eagerly peeled the paper wrapping from the caramels, "Tea is ready."

We all sat down at the kitchen table while Mammie poured cups of strong, steaming tea. Pappie brought out the lemon sponge cake and we children happily munched our candy, listening to the conversation around the table.

One memorable visit, I sat next to Tante Soof at the table. She and Mammie caught up on neighborhood news while Pappie listened and occasionally nodded his head. As Tante Soof stirred her tea, I noticed a small, reddish scar about two inches long on the white inner flesh of her forearm. Momentarily distracted from my cake, I reached out and ran my finger over the scar. It felt a little bumpy.

"Tante Soof, where did you get this scar?" I asked.

Tante Soof halted in mid-sentence. She looked down at me, then at Mammie and Pappie. Mammie's brows were tightly knitted together. She looked worried. The two sisters seemed to be carrying on a conversation with their eyes.

"I think she should know," Tante Soof said to Mammie, "You can't hide the truth forever."

Mammie said nothing. She looked down at her tea, stirring thoughtfully. Tante Soof began to speak.

The memory of those visits never fails to bring back the feeling of warmth and security I was fortunate to know as a child. Along with my affection for Tante Soof grew a great respect. At my parents' kitchen table at *Vredehoop*, Tante Soof told her story. It would stay with me the rest of my life.

"The heart of her husband trusteth in her, and he shall have no lack of gain."

CHAPTER 1

THE SOUND OF POPPING GLASS muffled by a cloth napkin was subdued compared to the joyous shouts of *"Mazel tov!"* that immediately followed. Forty-two year old Jan Rijnfeld lifted the veil to find Sofie's smiling lips awaiting his kiss. He gave her a perfunctory peck, slightly embarrassed under the watchful eyes of the guests, then placed her hand in the crook of his arm and whisked her away from beneath the *chuppah*. As the newlyweds made their way up the aisle of the synagogue, *Mevrouw* DeVries shook her head and leaned toward *Mevrouw* Cohen, seated in the pew in front of her.

"She doesn't know what she's getting herself into," whispered *Mevrouw* DeVries, "Filling the shoes of a dead wife is no picnic."

"And raising someone else's children … six, no less! Well, Sofie's a nice girl, but a beauty she isn't. And at her age, she can't afford to be too particular."

They clucked their tongues ruefully in agreement.

Sofie knew that people thought she was foolish to start life as a bride with six teenage stepdaughters. Even her own mother had doubts. But in Sofie, Jan's daughters found a caring, giving woman who filled the

13

maternal void they'd felt since their mother's death five years before.

Jopie, 21 and the eldest, found a friend in her new stepmother. She discovered that Sofie was easy to talk to and Jopie confided in her often, especially about her boyfriend David. He was a university student in Amsterdam and they planned to marry next year when he graduated. David intended to join his father's fur business, and Sofie and Jan were delighted that Jopie's future seemed secure.

Carla, age 19, was a pretty girl with light brown curls and a sweet smile. She worked as a stenographer in a Maarssen law office. Shy and reserved, she wasn't a girl who received a lot of attention from boys. She was glad that her father had remarried, for she knew how lonely he'd been in the years since cancer had claimed her mother.

Eighteen year old Lena was the beauty of the six sisters, and the most egregious. She had wheat-blonde hair that she was forever styling after her latest favorite film star. This month it was parted on the side with finger waves framing her heart-shaped face in an imitation of American actress Carole Lombard. Her hazel eyes were fringed with thick brown lashes and her smile was punctuated with a dimple on either side. She had graduated from high school a month before her father's marriage to Sofie, and now she was planning to take a secretarial course.

At 16, Elli was a devout bookworm. She loved school and spent most of her free time reading. Lena teased her mercilessly about her lack of social life, but quiet Elli was unperturbed. She was content to let her older sister be the social butterfly, while she lay sprawled on the sofa with her latest library find, twirling a lock of dark brown hair around her finger.

Often her peaceful solitude was broken when 14 year old Anneke came in and switched on the radio. With the perverse timing of little sisters, Anneke always seemed to have a burning desire to listen to the radio and practice the latest dance steps whenever Elli was deep in her book. Inevitably, Elli realized that Anneke wasn't going to heed the warning looks she gave her, and she flounced out of the room to seek sanctuary in her bedroom. Anneke blithely continued her Lindy, anxious to master it before Pappie came home and made her turn off the radio in favor of homework.

Eleven year old Mirjam was the only one of Jan's daughters who was unsure about her father's new marriage. Mirjam had been only six when her mother died, and she had few memories of her. Jopie and Carla had taken on the roles of mother surrogates, and Jan spent as much time at home as he could. Mirjam felt loved and secure, and couldn't understand why things in the family had to change. She resented Sofie and was jealous of her place in Jan's affections. Morosely, she watched her father and his new bride dancing.

"Mirjam, darling, come dance with us!" Sofie urged her youngest stepdaughter to join in the *hora*, the lively folk dance traditionally included in Jewish weddings.

Mirjam sighed and reluctantly clasped hands with Sofie on one side and Elli on the other, forming a large circle with the other dancers. Her woebegone look was not lost on Sofie, who understood the little girl's feelings. She smiled to herself as she thought that, eight months earlier, who would have guessed that today she would be dancing at her own wedding and the mother of six daughters?

It had been in March on a beautiful spring day in Amsterdam. Sofie got off the tram a few blocks ahead of her stop near DeBijekorf, the department store where she was a sales clerk in the glove department. She walked along the canal, enjoying the warm sunshine and the newly sprouting tulips.

Just then, a man walked up beside her and caught her hand. At Sofie's startled gasp, he quickly smiled and said, "Please, play along with me for a moment. I'll explain as we walk."

Too surprised even to withdraw her hand, Sofie looked at him. He had a nice face, with dark eyes and a reddish-brown moustache the color of an autumn leaf. He looked to be approaching middle age. She couldn't see his hair underneath his hat, but she imagined it was the same color as his moustache.

Still loosely holding her hand, the man introduced himself as Jan Rijnfeld. "I apologize for such *chutzpah*," he said, "but I was in something of a fix. I've been a widower for almost five years, and lately my mother has been playing matchmaker. She's determined to find me a new wife."

"And you don't want to remarry." Sofie concluded rather than inquired.

"Oh, I have nothing against the idea. In fact, I would like to give my girls — I have six — a mother-figure. I just want to be the one to choose the right time and the right woman."

Jan gestured toward a young woman wearing glasses and a decidedly unattractive hat, sitting primly on a bench by the canal.

"See that very proper lady in the red hat on the bench? I've been avoiding her for weeks. My mother seems to think we'd make a great couple. When I noticed her sitting there, I suddenly got the idea that if she saw me … well, with someone else, she'd give up conspiring with Mother."

"So you pretended I'm your ladyfriend," Sofie said.

"I'm sorry. I know it was a forward thing to do. I hope I haven't made you angry."

Sofie hesitated. "I don't know … I don't relish being grabbed by strangers, and I don't particularly enjoy dissembling."

There was contrition in Jan's voice. "I didn't mean to make you uncomfortable. Please forgive me.

May I escort you wherever you're headed? Please. I'd like to prove I'm not a complete louse."

Sofie was about to refuse, but something in his voice told her that he was not a masher. Besides, it was such a lovely day …

"Well … just as far as DeBijekorf," Sofie consented, "That's where I work."

"Thank you, *Juffrouw* … ?"

"Mecklenberg. Sofie Mecklenberg. And we'd better get going or I'll be late."

"Don't worry about that, *Juffrouw* Mecklenberg. I promise you won't be reprimanded for tardiness."

Sofie looked skeptical. "Now, how can you make such a promise? Do you know the store manager or something?

"I am the store manager," he smiled, tucking Sofie's hand in the crook of his arm.

On the day Jan brought Sofie to meet his daughters, she stood fussing before the mirror. Her hair was askew from trying on dress after dress. Nothing seemed right for the occasion. The tailored blue suit looked well on her, but it was too stiff and formal. She wanted to look easygoing and approachable when she met Jan's family. The grey pleated skirt and linen blouse were casual enough, but overemphasized her plump figure.

"Stop it, Sofie!" she chided herself in the mirror, "Look at you! Thirty-six years old and as nervous as a schoolgirl going to her first dance."

Selecting the skirt and blouse, she decided that she was what she was. If Jan accepted her that way, then his girls would, too. Stepping into the stylish black T-strap pumps she had brought home yesterday from DeBijekorf, she surveyed herself in the mirror. She turned around and swiveled her head to check her stocking seams in the mirror. Taking the comb from her dresser, she smoothed her flyaway hair into place. Once again, she mentally chided herself for being so nervous.

Though she was always neatly dressed and groomed, Sofie was not one to fuss over her appearance. She knew she was no glamour girl, and for years the Maarssen *yentas* had continually shaken their heads over her single status. But Sofie paid their wagging tongues no mind. She had been taught by her parents over the years that inner beauty is far more important than outward appearances. Consequently, Sofie grew up with a healthy self-esteem and an air of confidence that made her well-liked. Unfortunately, it seemed that most of the young men in Maarssen appreciated a shapely figure and a pretty face more than a kind heart and ready wit.

Then she met Jan. From the start, Jan made Sofie feel beautiful, outside and in. They spent every weekend together, taking long walks by the river and throwing bread to the ducks that gathered on its banks. They went to the cinema and shared a bag of candy while watching the latest American film. Jan laughingly told her that he had to keep up with Hollywood film stars or he would never know which one his daughter Lena was trying to copy.

When Jan came to dinner at Sofie's house, her parents sensed that a serious romance was blossoming.

"Be careful, Sofie," her mother cautioned, "Jan is a lovely man, but he has six children. Do you really want to take on a burden like that?"

Sofie turned a deaf ear to her mother's words. She was in love with

Jan and didn't want to dwell on anything that might mar her happiness …

She listened for the crunching sound of Jan's bicycle tires as he braked to a stop in the gravel driveway. Though she would not admit it, Sofie was a little frightened at the possibility of becoming a stepmother. She had no experience with children, having only an older sister.

Before she had time to think further, she heard the raucous call of the bulbous rubber horn attached to the handlebars of Jan's bicycle. They often rode the bicycle instead of Jan's car, particularly on balmy days like this one. After one last quick inspection in the mirror, she went down to meet him. Her new shoes squeaked on the stairs, but her heart was hammering so loudly that she didn't notice.

Jan smiled when he saw her. Sofie smiled back and took a deep breath. "I'm ready," she said.

They said goodbye to Sofie's parents and Jan helped her climb onto the small seat on the back of his bicycle. Sitting side-saddle, she put her arms around Jan's waist to keep her place on the small seat as Jan pedaled down the bumpy road. Sofie thought it very romantic, and was glad for an excuse to hold Jan close.

"Nervous?" he asked before they started down the road.

"A little. How can you tell?"

"You keep smoothing your skirt and running your hand over your hair. That's not like you, Soof."

Sofie smiled at the nickname Jan had bestowed on her. She liked the sense of intimacy it implied, as if they shared a secret. "I just want to make a good impression. What will the girls think of me?"

"They'll love you as much as I do."

Jan steered the bicycle to the side of the road and braked to a halt. Bracing one foot on the ground, he turned in his seat to look at Sofie. Taking her chilly hands in his warm ones, he said, "I do love you, Soof. I want us to be married."

Sofie's eyes became moist. She had wanted to hear Jan say those words for some time, ever since she knew she had fallen in love with him. Now, for the first time, she could tell him her true feelings.

Sofie circled her arms around his neck and kissed him. "Jan Rijnfeld, you're a fine man. And you know what? I love you, too."

Wiping tears from her eyes, she said, "Let's go meet the girls. We have a lot to tell them!" Sofie's laughter was light-hearted as Jan pedaled toward his home.

Sofie was warmly received by Jan's daughters, who had heard a good deal about this woman with whom their father had been spending so much time. Only Mirjam, the youngest, hung back when Sofie was introduced. Jan was a trifle embarrassed by this unusual display of shyness, but Sofie later explained to him that the little girl was bound to feel hesitant toward a new woman in her father's life.

After all, she said as they bicycled back to Sofie's house at evening's end, Mirjam had already lost her mother. She didn't want to lose her father, too.

Jan marveled at Sofie's understanding of Mirjam's feelings and her unconditional acceptance. Another woman might have been put off by the girl's cold reception. One of the things Jan loved best about Sofie was her generous heart.

Jan slowed to a stop on the driveway and put down the kickstand. Helping Sofie down, he said, "I'd like to come in and speak to your parents."

Sofie smiled. "They've probably already gone to bed, but for this I know they won't mind if we wake them."

She leaned toward him and their lips met. It was many minutes before they finally went inside.

Sofie and Jan had decided on a brief weekend honeymoon in Brussels. As they left the still-lively wedding reception to change into their traveling clothes, Carla Rijnfeld noticed Mirjam's chin beginning to tremble.

"What's wrong, Mirjam?"

"I don't want Pappie to go," Mirjam said, trying to keep her voice steady.

"But it's only for the weekend. And when he comes back, we'll have Soof as our new mother."

Carla and her sisters had adopted the nickname their father had given Sofie, and now the whole family called her "Soof."

"I don't want another mother. Just Pappie," Mirjam said.

Carla was concerned. She understood her littlest sister's jealousy of Soof, but she was very fond of her new stepmother and wanted her adjustment to a large, ready-made family to be as smooth as possible.

"She just wants to be your friend, Mirjam. She isn't going to try to take Mammie's place."

Mirjam sniffed and Carla realized that this was not a good time to talk sense to a confused 11 year old. Over the weekend, she and Jopie would have a heart-to-heart with Mirjam, but for now, Carla put a comforting arm around the little girl's shoulders.

Jan and Soof emerged in their "going away" clothes, all smiles. A carnation corsage perched on the lapel of Soof's new wool suit with the peplumed jacket. Jan looked dapper in a classic navy suit, white shirt, and dark tie. There were more shouts of *"Mazel tov!"* and slaps on the back for Jan as they made their way to the car waiting to take them to the train station.

Sofie's mother dabbed at her eyes with a handkerchief. Her father took Sofie's hands in his own and said, *"Sei gesund."* He kissed his daughter on both cheeks and shook Jan's hand.

"Be happy!" Soof's mother called as the car pulled away from the curb, her handkerchief fluttering her goodbye.

Mirjam sat at the kitchen table doing her homework. Though she had a desk in the bedroom she shared with Anneke, she preferred to study in the warmth of the kitchen. She felt lonely upstairs in her room, isolated from the rest of the family.

She chewed the tip of her fountain pen as she struggled with her assignment. *Mevrouw* Van Der Wal had instructed the class to write a composition on "The Person I Most Admire." Mirjam was having a hard time thinking of a subject for her theme. She admired Pappie a great deal, but it was boring to write about your own father. Queen Wilhelmina would make a good subject, but her best friend Bloeme was planning to write about the Queen. Mirjam's feathery brown eyebrows came together in consternation.

"What's that you're working on, Mirjam?"

Mirjam raised her head and eyed her stepmother. In the weeks since her parents had returned from their honeymoon, Mirjam still hadn't warmed up very much toward Soof. Despite Carla's and Jopie's efforts to reassure their sister that she wasn't losing a father but gaining a friend, Mirjam couldn't bring herself to soften towards her new stepmother.

Sofie told herself to give the girl time; losing a mother at so young an age must be very traumatic. She made a conscious effort not to overwhelm Mirjam with too much demonstrative affection in these first weeks, lest it be misconstrued as contrived and false. She wanted Mirjam to decide for herself that Soof was now part of the family.

She attempted to draw the little girl out by offering to help with her homework. "May I see what you're writing, darling?"

Mirjam covered the writing tablet with her arms.

"I haven't written anything yet," she said sullenly. "The teacher told us to write a composition about the person we most admire, but I can't think of anybody."

"Well now, that shouldn't be too hard. Maybe if we put our heads together, we can come up with an idea." Soof reached out for the pen in Mirjam's hand.

Mirjam snatched her hand away from Soof's reach, knocking to the ground as she did so the pitcher of milk still on the table from dinner.

At the sound of shattering glass, Jan came in from the other room, cigarette in hand. "What's going on?" he asked, "I heard a terrific racket."

Mirjam's horrified eyes went from the shards of glass and puddles of milk on the kitchen floor to her father to Soof. Her heart began to thump in grim anticipation of her father's reaction, not so much to the broken pitcher but to the truth of her behavior toward Soof, as Mirjam was sure she'd tell him.

Quickly, Soof gave a tinkling laugh and went to stand behind Mirjam's chair. "Oh, Jan, such a klutz you married! I knocked the pitcher off the table. What a mess! Mirjam was sweet enough to offer to help me clean up." She rested her hands on Mirjam's shoulders.

Jan's eyes crinkled in a smile. One of the qualities he loved best about Soof was her cheerful attitude. Nothing seemed to dampen her good spirits.

He stubbed out his cigarette in the ashtray on the living room table and gingerly crossed the kitchen floor.

"Come, we'll all clean up together."

Jan started picking up the larger pieces of broken glass while Sofie began mopping up the spilled milk.

For a long moment, Mirjam just stood there, staring at her stepmother. Sofie was so engrossed in her task that she didn't notice Mirjam kneel beside her on the floor until the girl touched her arm. With tears brimming in her brown eyes, she handed Soof the dry rags she had silently fetched from the pantry. Soof smiled at her and enfolded Mirjam in a fierce hug. Without a word, Soof and Mirjam came to a new understanding. Only much later would Mirjam realize how she had almost alienated the one person on whom she would come to depend for her very survival.

*"She looketh well to the ways
of her household, And eateth
not the bread of idleness"*

CHAPTER 2

THE NEXT THREE YEARS WERE HAPPY ones for
the Rijnfeld family. Sofie joyfully threw herself into her role as wife
and mother, making Jan's large house in Amsterdam a happier place
than it had been in many a year. Sofie found it all very gratifying,
and she frequently reminded her mother how wrong she had been
to caution her daughter against taking on an instant family. Sofie's
new daughters quickly warmed to the love and nurturing she brought
to their home, and Mirjam grew especially close to her stepmother,
which pleased Jan considerably.

As he walked home from the tram stop one balmy evening in
May, he thought about all the blessings that had come to rest on his
doorstep. DeBijekorf had promoted Jan to district manager, which
involved frequent travel to the various stores in his territory. He never
worried about his family during these absences, knowing everything
at home was in Soof's capable hands. He enjoyed his new job and
was grateful to Soof for her support.

When he had first learned of the impending promotion, he had
discussed its pros and cons with his wife. She knew how much this

new position meant to Jan and she urged him to take it, telling him not to worry about being on the road.

Though he wouldn't admit as much, Jan was relieved at Sofie's agreement. He had previously been a contender for this promotion the first year after his wife died but had been forced to decline, knowing he could not be away so much from home and his motherless girls. It would not have been good for Anneke and Mirjam, particularly, and it would not have been fair to burden Jopie and Carla with the responsibility of homemaking and mothering the young ones. Though his position as manager of the Amsterdam store had been a comfortable one, he had regretted the necessary stagnation in his career.

Now it seemed the world was his oyster. He had found love anew, his career was on the rise, and he had a happy family once again. Even as he mused on his good fortune, he shivered with a kind of foreboding. He had so many blessings to be thankful for … when was the other shoe going to drop?

The rise of Nazism in Germany and the invasion of Poland the previous year had made Jan and all European Jews wary of the future. Over the past seven years, hundreds of German Jews had emigrated to Holland to escape Hitler's persecution. Jopie's girlfriend Miep worked for one of them, a Frankfurt man who had uprooted his wife and two young daughters from Hitler's Germany to start a new life in Amsterdam. Now he owned a profitable fruit pectin factory, and his family was free to live as they pleased. Surely Holland was safe from Hitler's menacing hand, or why would so many Jews have sought refuge here?

As he approached the house, Jan shook his head to disperse the unpleasantness that pricked his mind. He dwelled on things too much. When his mind started rambling like this, he could work himself into such a state that he'd be almost afraid to relax and enjoy. The thought of losing any part of his new life might prove more than he could bear.

Jan opened the front door to a tumult of chattering and squealing. Jopie was standing in the midst of her sisters and stepmother, and everybody was talking at once.

24

Sofie caught sight of her husband standing in the entryway and broke away from the circle of excited girls.

"What's going on?" Jan asked as she kissed him in greeting.

Sofie's eyes danced. "Jopie and David are engaged! He gave her a ring this afternoon."

Jan's moustache spread upward into a broad smile as he made his way over to the excited group, clamoring for a look at Jopie's left hand.

Jopie saw her father and excitedly held up her hand for him to see. "Oh, Pappie, look, look! Isn't it gorgeous?"

A 1.7-carat solitaire set in a simple platinum band sparked fire as Jopie moved her hand around in the sunbeams coming in through the window.

High time, Jan thought to himself.

David Davidson had been working alongside his father for the past two years, learning the furrier's trade. Now he was firmly established as heir apparent to Davidson's Furs, and the "understanding" between him and Jopie Rijnfeld at last could be made official.

Jan kissed his daughter's cheek and joined in the excitement of the occasion.

"May 9, 1940," he declared dramatically, "The day my first-born became engaged. A date to remember!"

Sofie herded the family into the kitchen where dinner was waiting. She enjoyed cooking, and had prepared a traditional *Shabbat* meal. Even though neither Jan nor Sofie were particularly religious, lighting the sabbath candles and having what Sofie called "a good Jewish meal" on Friday nights were rituals in the Rijnfeld household. Mirjam lit the candles while Sofie recited the blessing: *baruch atah Adonai elohenu melech ha'olam* ...

This *Shabbat* dinner was much the same as on previous Friday nights: homemade chicken soup with matzo balls, roast chicken, Swiss chard, new potatoes with parsley butter. But tonight's meal had a festive air about it, making it seem more like a Passover or *Rosh Hashana* meal. Jopie's engagement had made this a very special *Shabbat*, indeed.

And Sofie had so much to think about! This wedding would be her first important role as a hostess, and she looked forward to making all the happy plans with Jopie. There was the trousseau to buy and new dresses for all the girls … what fun they would have shopping! Tomorrow was Saturday; they would go to DeBijekorf first thing …

The Davidsons called on the Rijnfelds that evening after supper to toast their newly engaged children. The ring was admired further and everyone had some champagne, including 14 year old Mirjam.

Everyone also had his or her own idea of how and when the wedding should take place. Jopie thought an autumn wedding would be nice. David's mother thought autumn weddings conflicted too much with the High Holy Days; a summer wedding was much more practical. Anyway, June is the traditional month for brides.

David's father pointed out that they barely even observed the Holy Days, so just how would a wedding interfere? Elli chimed in that Soof couldn't possibly plan a big wedding in so short a time. Jopie politely asked Elli to stay out of it; it wasn't for her to speak for Soof or to assume that Jopie even wanted a big wedding, for that matter.

David said that if there was going to be such a fuss, he and Jopie would just elope and call it a day. Jan said they would do no such thing; he had looked forward all his life to the *naches* of walking his first-born down the aisle, and he was not going to be denied that privilege …

It was late by the time the Davidsons left. Sofie and Jan slowly climbed the stairs to their room, elated but weary.

"What a day!" Soof sighed, "Jopie is positively glowing!"

"Isn't she?" Jan concurred proudly, "She'll make a beautiful bride."

"There hasn't been this much excitement around here since our own engagement. I doubt if Jopie will sleep a wink tonight. Or me either, for that matter!"

"We've got a bright future ahead of us, Soof."

"We surely do. But you know something, Jan? I wouldn't care if we lost everything tomorrow. We have each other and our daughters … far more riches than most people can claim in a lifetime."

In answer, Jan put his arm around his wife and gave her a little hug. That cold finger of fear that had touched him earlier as he had walked home from the tram stop now returned. He couldn't pinpoint the source of his uneasiness, but he decided not to dwell on it, wanting nothing to diminish the joy of this day. He gave a mental shrug as he followed Soof into their bedroom and closed the door behind them.

BOOM!

In the pre-dawn darkness, Soof was startled out of sleep by a terrific thundering noise.

BOOM!

She sat upright in bed as the door flew open and all six girls ran in, their eyes wide with fright. At the next deafening roar, Anneke screamed and clapped her hands over her ears, squeezing her eyes shut. Lena put a comforting arm around her sister's shoulders, though she felt like screaming, too.

"What on earth is that?" Soof asked in a panic-stricken voice.

"It sounds like bombs," Jan said cautiously, not wanting to add to his family's mounting fear.

Mirjam gasped at her father's words. "Bombs? she shrieked, Are we going to die?"

Carla enfolded Mirjam in her arms, as much from her own need for security as to reassure her little sister.

Jan threw off the bedclothes and started for the stairs.

"The radio. That should tell us what's going on."

The family followed Jan down the stairs to the living room where the large radio stood against the far wall. But when Jan turned the knob and waited the minute or so it took the radio to warm up — a minute, which seemed an eternity to the anxious Rijnfelds — all they heard was static. No help there.

"Soof, gather up some blankets and a jug of water. We'll go down cellar until we can find out what's going on. The bombs —"

He stopped in mid-sentence and changed his next words.

"Power must be temporarily out. I'm sure in a while we'll be able to hear something."

Quietly and quickly, Soof had the girls gather up all the quilts from their beds and the extra blankets in the linen closet while she filled pitchers and jugs with water. The family waited down in the cool, dim cellar for the next two hours, watching as the brightening day shone in through the small rectangular window cut high in the eastern wall.

At last, the thunderings ceased. All that could be heard were the sounds of the birds perched in the linden tree in the front yard, chirping as though nothing extraordinary had happened.

When Jan felt it was safe, they emerged from the cellar, blinking at the bright sunlight streaming in the living room windows. They gathered around the radio as Jan turned the knob once more. This time they were rewarded by a crackle and then a voice speaking rapidly but calmly.

Germany had invaded Holland and the Low Countries. Air attacks had begun at five thirty that morning, with German infantry progressing up the Yssel River, 10 miles from the Germany-Netherlands border. In addition to shelling in various locations, German stormtroopers were parachuting into Holland. Already, though, French and British forces were crossing the border to help the Dutch and Belgian armies withstand the shock of at least 29 German divisions making their way to these newest conquests.

Netherlanders were warned, however, that German parachutists could be dressed in Allied uniforms to fool unsuspecting citizens. Even worse, they were known to disguise themselves as farm hands and Roman Catholic nuns.

"Good God," whispered Sofie.

The announcer went on to say that all schools would be closed that day, and all public amusements in Amsterdam were canceled. Citizens were urged to remain calm and to stay tuned to their radios for continued information.

All that long day, Jan, Sofie, and the girls remained huddled around the radio. A broadcast message from the mayor of the Hague reminded citizens of the laws forbidding advances in prices under such circumstances. Exchanges were closed and would remain so, but payments by Netherlands Bank and private banks would be uninterrupted. The newspaper reported that some runs on commercial banks had taken place, but all withdrawals were met in cash. Jan was somewhat reassured by this news, feeling that if Holland's financial affairs were intact, the situation hadn't deteriorated into complete mayhem.

Telephone communications were curtailed, with no outgoing international calls permitted. Business was generally at a standstill, and a complete blackout was ordered for that night. Sofie, Jopie, and Carla collected the thickest quilts and nailed them into the walls above the window frames. The sides and bottoms were secured with thumbtacks so that during the day the quilts could be folded back to let in the light.

For five long days the Dutch bravely fought against the German attackers. Sofie and her family listened to a radio message broadcast by the British Minister to the Netherlands, who assured them of Britain's continued alliance. Reports were heard of German stormtroopers in their insidious disguises floating to the ground under graceful ballooning parachutes, only to land in a circle of Dutch soldiers, their bayoneted rifles simultaneously pointing inward.

Such victories were small, but were victories nonetheless — even sweeter when one considered the lengths to which the Germans had gone to deceive the Dutch. Citizens were cautioned to be wary of uniformed personnel; what appeared to be a soldier of the Allies could very well be a soldier of the Reich in disguise.

The perfidy of the German army was limitless. Over several towns planes jettisoned pamphlets containing deliberately falsified information and hollow threats against the civilian population, a measure designed to cause confusion and panic among the Dutch and enhance their vulnerability.

Jan warned Sofie and the girls not to fall prey to these tactics. They must remember that the information in those pamphlets was a sham, the threats empty.

"But, Pappie, how do you know for sure? Maybe they really mean what they say," questioned Lena.

"I know. *Zayde* used to tell me stories of what the Germans did in the Great War ... they were no less underhanded. They want to give us a good scare so we'll give up without too much of a fight. But they underestimate Netherlanders," answered Jan confidently.

Unfortunately, Jan's confidence was not enough to overthrow the German army, who greatly outnumbered the Dutch. By the end of the siege, Queen Wilhelmina and the royal family had sought refuge in England, along with the Dutch government. The Netherlands had fallen.

Half a world away in America, the war in Europe had an unreal quality, too distant to have much of an impact on the thousands of people who had come to New York City from all over the country to attend the May 11th opening of the World's Fair.

As far as Emily and Russell Metcalf were concerned, there was no war, no throngs milling about the fairgrounds, no one else in the busy city but the two of them. For a newly-married couple on their honeymoon, life held nothing but happiness.

They stood at the corner, waiting for the traffic light to change so they could cross the street. Russell took advantage of the moment to give Emily a long kiss, much to the amusement of the other pedestrians around them. Their embrace was interrupted by the rhythmic hawking of the paperboy standing next to the light post.

"PA-pers! GET your papers here! READ all a-BOUT it ... 'Dutch and Belgians Resist Nazi Drive' ... Extra! Extra!"

The boy held up a *New York Times* while several customers stood nearby, noses deep in their papers. Emily looked at them curiously.

"Something big must be going on, Russell. Everybody's devouring the newspaper like it's the end of the world or something. Did I hear the paperboy say something about the Nazis?"

"Oh, yeah. In addition to our wedding — which, in my opinion, was the most important world event to take place yesterday — the

Germans invaded Holland and Belgium."

"Oh, dear, no. Those poor people ... "

Emily lowered her head, thinking what the news of the invasion must mean to Europe. Then a new thought came to her.

"Russell, you don't think America will get involved, do you?" she asked.

"I doubt it, honey. Britain and France have already gone in to help the Dutch and Belgians ... we won't need to get into it."

"And how do you know so much about it?" Emily teased, "Aren't you the guy who said that the only thing he's interested in is me?"

"Well, with you taking so long in the bathroom getting ready this morning, I had to do something to kill time. I heard it on the radio while you were in the tub."

"Let's buy a paper, Russell. I want to know what's going on. This may affect our future!"

Russell smiled. Dramatic Emily. Indulgently, he let his pretty wife drag him over to the paperboy. He handed him a nickel and took a paper from the stack, then led Emily to a vacant spot near the semaphore.

The light changed and a crowd of pedestrians moved of one accord down the curb and across the street, but the Metcalfs remained behind. Russell opened the paper and Emily leaned against him to read, one arm around his waist, her head close to his. As they read the accounts of the German parachute drops, Emily tried to imagine what it would be like to have the enemy drift into your world like snowflakes falling from the sky ... to have the deafening sound of exploding bombs rip you out of a peaceful sleep ...

"Oh, Russell, what if America declares war on Germany? They'll draft you!"

Russell was patient as he reassured her. "No, Em, this is a European war. FDR doesn't want to get involved and I'm not going anywhere. So stop borrowing trouble." He gave her an affectionate nudge. "C'mon, Em, cheer up. This is the only honeymoon we'll ever have, so let's go have some fun. We'll solve the world's problems later." Russell tossed the paper into a wire trash bin.

All that day, Emily could not get her mind off the invasion. She imagined newlyweds — just like they were — in Holland or Belgium whose honeymoon had changed from a beautiful dream into some kind of unreal nightmare. A nagging depression dogged her for the next few days until Russell was able to jolly her out of her glum mood.

By the time they returned to their small apartment in Boston, she had all but forgotten the war and how upset she had been over Hitler's latest conquests. Russell went back to work at the architectural firm of Kirk & Neumann, where he had first met Emily, a secretary to one of the junior partners. At Russell's insistence, she had given notice at the firm and spent her time fixing up the apartment.

Content with her new job as a wife, Emily's world consisted of happy days turning the apartment into a home, and cozy evenings at home with Russell. There was no room in her world for distressing thoughts on the war in Europe. When you're young and in love, it seems as if nothing will ever change.

"She doeth him good
and not evil,
all the days of her life"

CHAPTER 3

IN THE SEVEN MONTHS SINCE the German invasion
of Holland, the tranquil lives of the Rijnfelds and all other Dutch Jews
were little affected by the occupation. This came as a great surprise to
Sofie and Jan, who had heard stories of the Nazis' treatment of Jews
in Germany and Poland. When they heard about ghettos and random
killings of Jews and others whom the Nazi regime had classified as
"unacceptable," Sofie and Jan found it hard to comprehend. In fact,
most of the Jews in Amsterdam, Maarssen, and all over the Netherlands
felt that surely such stories must be exaggerated. Unlike the rest of
Europe, Dutch Jews were quite assimilated into mainstream society and
unaccustomed to persecution.

"The Germans are a civilized people. They wouldn't debase
themselves to such behavior," said Frieda Davidson, pouring coffee into a
delicate china cup, which she handed to her husband.

The Davidsons had invited the entire Rijnfeld family to their house
to celebrate David's birthday. They had coffee and cake in the Davidsons'
living room while they discussed the events that had transpired since the
invasion.

Hans Davidson took the cup from his wife and set it before him on the coffee table. He leaned back into the sofa cushions in order to reach deep into his trousers pocket. He drew out a slightly tarnished brass pillbox, took two saccharin tablets from it and dropped them into his coffee. They dissolved in a fizzy eruption of foam. Hans stirred the coffee with his spoon.

"For once, Frieda and I agree."

His wife shot him a look of warning, which he ignored.

"Germany is a country of humanism. No other country in Europe can touch them for culture, intellectualism, academic excellence … "

"Academic excellence which has bred the very intellectuals who masterminded the Reich's plan to conquer Europe," Jan pointed out.

"How do you mean? Because they parachuted into Holland disguised as nuns?" Hans' rotund belly shook with laughter. "When it comes to war, Jan, Germany is no different from any other country. Check the history books. Enemies have always resorted to dissembling, even in fiction. Remember the Trojan Horse of Greek mythology?"

When Jan nodded, Hans went on. "Besides, it's not as though we're such an observant community. If the Nazis go after any Dutch Jews at all, they'll target the Orthodox and Hasidic."

"A Jew is a Jew, Papa," David put in.

Hans gave his son a skeptical look. "Think about it, David. The Nazis have been conditioned and have conditioned others to look at Jews as a caricature, a stereotype. Take a look at yourself: do you look any different from any gentile on the street?"

"No, of course not, but —"

"Then mark my words. Any harassment that might take place will happen only to any Jew fool enough to shout it to the world that he's a Jew. We'll be all right. You'll see."

For a time, Hans Davidson gloated in the truth of his arguments. In fact, he delighted in rubbing in an occasional "I told you so" to Jan, though he was careful not to overdo it and push his *machutten* too far. In deference to the children, he refrained from stirring up a hornet's nest.

When the news came that the *Führer* had released Dutch prisoners of war, even Jan began to think Hans had been right. Maybe Hitler intended to treat them fairly. The German news reports called it a magnanimous gesture, a sign of the *Führer's* good will toward the Dutch people.

Unbeknownst to Jan and the rest of the Netherlands, though, Hitler's release of the prisoners was merely a ploy to gain Holland's trust, to give them a false sense of security. Whatever the intent, the fact remained that the husbands, sons, brothers, and sweethearts who had been awaiting their fate in German prison camps were now home.

Hans Davidson's delight in proving the futility of Rijnfeld's skepticism partly assuaged the concern he had for some of the initial changes effected by the Germans, though he would never admit as much to Jan. Shortly after the invasion, the Germans centralized the Dutch labor exchanges, as well as the local Dutch department that granted unemployment and other benefits. This enabled the Germans to utilize Dutch labor for their own purposes. By the end of 1940, 89,000 Netherlanders were working in Germany, with another 30,000 in France and Belgium.

Despite the seemingly decent treatment by the Germans, 248 Dutch Jews committed suicide following the invasion. Most people couldn't understand such a drastic measure. Still ... did they know something that the rest of Holland's Jews didn't?

It wasn't until July of 1940 that the first anti-Jewish edicts were issued by the Germans. All Jews had to leave their positions in the air-raid precautions department. At the same time, all civil servants must sign an "Aryan Declaration," affirming their loyalty to the Party cause. Obviously, few Jewish civil servants would sign such a document, and those who refused were subsequently fired from their jobs.

By October, all Jewish-owned businesses were registered with the German authorities. By November, all Jewish civil servants who still remained in their positions were dismissed. However, they would receive 85 percent of their salaries for three months, 70 percent for the next five years, 60 percent for the following five years, and 50 percent for the rest of their lives.

As far as the Nazis were concerned, this bespoke of benevolence. See how well we treat you? When have a conquered people been dealt with so fairly?

Even Hans Davidson couldn't have known that the Nazis felt quite safe in making these concessions … safe in the knowledge that the half-salaries promised would never be delivered.

As the year came to a close, more and more limitations were placed on the Jews. Aryan girls were no longer permitted to work in domestic capacities for Jewish families. Public meetings were forbidden. The Dutch press was taken over by the Germans, and radio broadcasts were censored. Leiden University was closed in December, leaving hundreds of Jewish students with no way to complete their degrees.

Thus were Amsterdam's Jews gradually isolated. The scores of Jews who had worked in civil service lost the friends alongside whom they had worked for years, even decades. Civil servants had a strong sense of duty and were accustomed to following orders to the letter, and no one was willing to risk his own job for the sakes of displaced Jewish workers. If orders dictated disassociation with former Jewish co-workers, then so be it. After all, it wasn't as though the Jews were left destitute; the Germans had been more than generous in their financial settlement.

Oddly enough, the reaction of much of the Jewish community to these directives was one of little concern. Of the more than 140,000 Jews living in Holland, many maintained that there was nothing to worry about. What was happening in Germany couldn't possibly happen here.

There were some, however, who had sought refuge in Holland from Hitler's persecution in their own homelands. These Jews felt again the centuries-old feeling of being hunted. Their safe haven was not so safe, it now seemed. Had they jumped from the frying pan into the fire? A small minority saw a serious threat in the Nazi invasion of the Netherlands and fled the country, leaving everything behind. Purchasing false documents and identity cards, some escaped to Britain, others to America, and a handful to Palestine.

As 1940 became 1941, the anti-Jewish campaign systematically continued. By the second month of the new year, an order was issued for all Jews to register with the German authorities. Residents of Amsterdam were given two weeks to report; those living elsewhere in Holland were allotted four weeks.

The German definition of a Jew was a detail even Hans Davidson could not have predicted. Jews were divided into three categories:

Volljuden, full-blooded Jews; *Halbjuden*, half-blooded Jews; and *Vierteljuden*, those with only one quarter Jewish blood. All were mandated to register as Jews, even those who may have converted to Christianity.

On a cold day in late February, Jan and Sofie piled the girls into the sedan for the drive into Amsterdam. Jews must obtain registration cards, and the deadline was approaching for the Rijnfelds to obtain theirs, or face the consequences.

Consequences I don't care to find out, Jan thought. He remained as nonchalant as possible so as not to frighten the girls, but a knot of fear formed in his gut. The Nazi rein on the Jews was tightening, and Jan tried not to contemplate where it would lead to next. He still had his job, which was a blessing. Many of their friends and neighbors had long ago lost theirs. The Davidsons' fur business was registered with the authorities, but so far the Germans had left it alone. At least his family and his daughter's future in-laws were not suffering.

"Jan, I still think we should have taken the tram into the city. I'm afraid we'll call too much attention to ourselves in the car," Sofie fretted.

"No, Soof, it's freezing outside today. I wouldn't let you and girls stand around on a windy tram platform, getting frostbite," Jan said firmly.

He slowed the sedan as they neared the building the Germans had claimed for their headquarters and searched around for a place to park.

As luck would have it, there was a space across the street from the building.

Jan stopped the car in front of the entrance. "Soof, take the girls and get out here so you won't all have to climb over the dirty snow on the sidewalk. I'll park and join you in a minute."

Sofie got out of the car, followed by her stepdaughters. Mirjam's eyes grew round at the sight of the huge Nazi flag draped over the upper facade of the headquarters building. The black swastika looked ominous. Sofie took Mirjam's gloved hand in hers and squeezed it reassuringly. They crossed the street and waited for Jan in front of the large double doors.

He maneuvered the car forward and back and forward again until the sedan was suitably in place. As he got out of the car, a German Army jeep sped by, flinging bits of dirty city slush onto the front of Jan's coat. He heard the jeers of its occupants as he tried to brush off the wet mess. Crossing the street to where his family stood waiting, he saw the concerned look in Soof's eyes and the frightened ones of his daughters. He tried to make light of it as he herded them into the building.

The registration office was crowded with other Jews reporting for their identity cards. There were only a few benches lining the walls, and very little room to stand. Three long queues snaked their way around the small room, making it hard to tell which line was which.

Jan located the end of the line designated "M-Z" and took his place with Sofie and the girls right behind. The line seemed interminable. The closeness of the crowded room and the heavy winter coats they wore soon made them uncomfortably warm. They removed their coats and scarves, which helped a little.

Finally, their turn came. They stood before the small table where an officer sat with a ledger.

"Name?" he asked, without looking up.

"Rijnfeld, Jan."

"You have your family with you?"

"Yes. My wife and daughters."

The officer looked up at Jan, then scrutinized Sofie and the girls. He took down their names as Jan gave them and pulled out eight identical yellow cards. He dabbed a rubber stamp several times onto an inkpad, then methodically stamped each card with a large letter J. Watching with a calm she didn't really feel, Sofie felt as though they were calves being branded. Proof of ownership.

"All right, *Herr* Rijnfeld, that will be eight guilders," said the officer.

"I don't understand," said Jan, "We have to pay for these identity cards?"

The officer shook his head and snickered. "You Jews. Always want something for nothing, don't you?"

"But —"

"Eight guilders, *mach schnell!* We don't have all day," the officer barked.

Jan reached into his wallet and pulled out a ten guilder note.

Handing it to the officer, he waited for change. The officer waived Jan away and called out, "Next!"

A soldier pushed Jan aside to make room. The shove dominoed Jan into those waiting in the adjacent line. They immediately began to upbraid the Rijnfelds for causing the ruckus.

Jan ushered his family out into the hall as quickly as he could weave through the crowded room. Once outside the building, he heaved a sigh of relief. At least the ordeal was over.

Glad to be away from the stuffiness of the registration office, Sofie breathed deeply of the fresh cold air and relaxed at being out of that building. The ambience inside the Headquarters building had made her uncomfortable, and she hadn't realized how tense she was. Just then, she froze and touched Jan's arm. "Jan, the car!"

Jan looked across to where he had parked the sedan. It was no longer there. Now what? How could it have been stolen in broad daylight, in full view of the military?

"Stay here, everybody. I'll go inside and speak to someone about this."

Jan went back into the building and looked around, unsure which office to try first. He noticed a door marked *Administration*, and he turned the knob. Inside were two metal desks side by side, each occupied by a young German enlisted man.

They look no older than Lena, Jan thought.

Phones were ringing, even though both soldiers were already talking on their desk extensions, and Jan could hear the clackety-clack of a typewriter in the back. One of the soldiers finished his phone conversation and looked at Jan.

"You want something?"

"Yes, please. It seems my car has been stolen. I parked it right across the street not one hour ago, and now it's gone."

"Your papers, *bitte*."

It was a second or two before Jan understood what the soldier was talking about. He reached inside his coat pocket for the yellow registration card and handed it to him. The soldier examined it, looked up at Jan, and frowned at the card.

"Wait here," he told Jan and disappeared with the card into the back office.

The sounds of the typewriter stopped and Jan heard two voices speaking in German. A lieutenant emerged from the office with Jan's card in his hand. His face wore a smile but his eyes were steely as he looked at Jan.

"You wish to report a stolen vehicle?"

"Yes, Lieutenant. It's a black sedan with — "

"I don't need a description. The private will give you a form to fill out, but I'm not making any promises. Searching for missing autos is not a priority for the Reich."

The officer turned on his heel and went back to his office, closing the door none too gently behind him.

Jan knew it was useless to protest. He wouldn't get anywhere with these people.

He remembered that Soof and the girls must be freezing outside and hurried to where they waited. They turned to look at Jan expectantly. Anneke's nose was red.

"Well, Soof, I guess we'll be riding the tram after all," Jan said ruefully.

"What happened, Pappie? Are they going to look for the car?" asked Jopie.

"I filed a report on it, dear, but I doubt if they're going to look very hard."

The family crossed the street and headed for the tram station, anxious to get home. The cold was getting worse, and the stress of the excursion had drained them all. As they rounded the corner, Carla stopped in her tracks.

"Look!" she cried, pointing.

They all turned to see their black sedan, the unmistakable uniform of the S.S. on the man in the driver's seat. Sofie's eyes darted to the license plate, confirming what she already knew. She looked up at Jan, who sighed heavily but resumed walking.

"Come," he said, "Let's go home."

In light of the recent events, Jopie and David decided to postpone their June wedding. The trip to buy registration cards had frightened Jopie more than she had let on to her family. When she told David of the day's happenings, he agreed that they should hold off making plans until things calmed down a bit.

Perhaps by autumn, David consoled a tearful Jopie. Maybe the war would be over by then.

David's optimism was not to bear fruit. In protest of the stream of restrictions that continued to pour over the Jews, street fights broke out. This time, however, it was Dutch against Dutch: Jewish resistors versus Dutch Nazis.

Brawls became so commonplace that the Nazis formulated the Jewish Council, a leadership body responsible for maintaining calm and order in the Jewish community. This served the Nazis a twofold purpose: a means of controlling the fighting problem without detracting from the business of winning the war, and an excuse to hold the Jews responsible if they failed in their duty.

Of course, these Jews could not be trusted with weapons. They must surrender their firearms immediately.

How are we to keep the peace without weapons, the newly appointed Council asked.

That is your problem, replied the S. S. You Jews are supposed to be so intelligent; figure it out!

The occupation reached a climax on February 22nd — a Saturday and the Jewish Sabbath — when 425 young Jews were rounded up and transported to Mauthausen concentration camp in Austria.

These round-ups, known as *razzias,* were to become a source of terror to the Jews of Amsterdam. Any young people walking along the street were vulnerable to these sudden conscriptions. The Germans were known even to burst into Jewish homes and whisk away young members of the family.

In response to the first *razzias,* Amsterdam retaliated on February 25th with a city-wide strike of the railway and tram systems, city cleansing, and public works departments. Although its intentions were good, the strike only complicated life even further for the Jews. Once Jan Rijnfeld no longer had his automobile, he had relied on public transportation to get to work. Now he was forced to find some other way. Luckily, his bicycle had not yet been confiscated, so each day he pedaled the wet streets of Amsterdam to DeBijekorf, bundled up against the bitter wind that stung his face.

As winter melted into spring and spring wafted into summer, life in the Rijnfeld home continued on a fairly even keel. The passage of June left Jopie inconsolable, as the day her wedding should have taken place came and went much like any other day in German-occupied Holland.

The Germans, however, were making daily life more of a frightening ordeal for their captors. There were more *razzias*, and in one instance 300 Jewish men were rounded up and sent to Mauthausen. As the expense of the war depleted their coffers, the Germans began confiscating Jewish fortunes to cover their own expenditures. Dutch Jews of wealth and position were forced out of their homes and businesses, their valuables appropriated and moneys taken. As the frequency of *razzias* and other Nazi tactics escalated, the Jews became less and less inclined to protest, fearing repercussions. By September 1941, over 160,000 Dutch Jews were registered with the S. S., and identity cards had been issued for all.

Despite the war, Sofie was happy. She grew closer to her stepdaughters all the time, and began to forget that there had ever been a time in her life without them. Jan was a kind, gentle husband who gratefully abdicated much of his parental responsibilities to his willing wife. This was fortuitous, since Jan was so preoccupied with the political situation at hand that he became emotionally unavailable.

In the naive, self-centered way of teenagers, the Rijnfeld girls were largely unconcerned with the war and the goings-on around them. Jopie was caught up in wedding plans, despite the fact that they had not been able to set a firm date. Carla was just as absorbed, accompanying Jopie to look at fabrics and dress styles. She was still no more popular with boys than she had been when Sofie first met her, so she took a vicarious delight in her older sister's marriage plans.

Lena, on the other hand, had grown even prettier in the last few years, her blonde hair the color of wheat shimmering in the sun. She found the Occupation an annoying hindrance to her social life. Many of her girlfriends were warned by their parents not to walk outside after four o'clock in the afternoon, even though there was no such prohibition by the Nazis.

As her companions became less and less available, Lena found herself at home more than usual. Dates were few and far between. The young men who once swarmed around the Rijnfeld house were reluctant to venture far from their own doors, the danger of *razzias* ever present now. Serious Elli was still devoted to her books, grateful that the Germans hadn't made the public library off limits to her. She worked hard at her studies and, except for that other-worldly trip to the city to obtain their identity cards, her existence seemed much the same as it had before the war. Now and again she found herself noticing that some of the young German soldiers were very attractive, but she knew she would never meet these young men. She wasn't sure she even wanted to.

Anneke and Mirjam, the two youngest daughters, were also seemingly oblivious to the war. Still lively, still full of fun, Anneke missed the Saturday afternoons when she and a group of friends would go tea dancing at the Vanderhouck Hotel. Jews were no longer allowed there, so Anneke and her friends gathered at one or another's home and listened to the radio or played records on the gramophone. There was still fun to be had!

Mirjam was now 15, trying to become a young lady under the most difficult of circumstances. Growing up is never easy at best, but when the country is at war and under the enemy's thumb, it is a scary, puzzling business. Sofie was particularly protective of Mirjam, and kept her close to home. She had heard too many stories of German soldiers raping young Dutch girls found alone.

The last four years should have been ones of discovery and growth for Mirjam, as she turned from childhood to young womanhood. But there was only apprehension and fear. She never had the chance to go on a first date, to proudly wear silk stockings and high heels to her first party, to ride on a bicycle behind a shy boy and feel him tense with nervousness when she put her arms around his waist. She was interested in the boys at school, but budding flirtations began and ended there. It was a stifling existence for a young girl anxious to stretch her wings.

Nineteen forty-two rang in with the resonant bells of the great Westertoren clock that towered above the buildings of Amsterdam. The impact of the war could really be felt now. Food rationing was implemented, with quality and quantity both on the decline. Ersatz coffee, tea, and tobacco were available for those who tried to convince themselves that they actually tasted like the real thing. The advent of these substitutes was an attempt to retain the illusion of taste, but the taste had gone out of life for the Dutch.

Almost imperceptibly, life as the Jews of Holland knew it was taken away. Little by little, new mandates were issued that chipped away at the freedom of the Jews. All stores and businesses belonging to Jews were closed. No Jews were allowed to drive cars. No telephone usage was permitted.

A curfew of eight o'clock p.m. was imposed on the Jews. Then it was shortened to six p.m. Eventually it was forbidden to sit on any balconies facing the street. Ultimately, it was decreed that Jews were not allowed outside their homes at all, except in the late afternoon from three o'clock to five o'clock to buy food, which they could purchase only from the few Jewish-owned shops allowed to remain open. Naturally, this resulted in a shopping frenzy. The local market where Sofie bought her groceries was soon emptied. The grocer simply gave away what little stock he had left.

Once the Germans saw that the Dutch offered little or no resistance to their directives, they escalated them until they had complete martial control. Violators of the New Order would be shot. Jews were now ordered to turn in all valuables: bicycles, jewelry, silver, foreign currency, precious stones. They may keep only wedding rings, watches, and the gold in their teeth. A knife, fork, and two spoons may also be retained.

Jews were raped materially and religiously, for among the valuables in every Jewish household were *Shabbat* candlesticks and *Kiddush* cups. In some families, these objects had been handed down from generation to generation, their sentimental value more priceless than their silver content. Even the poorest of Jewish families had silver candlesticks or *Kiddush* cups. Those who were clever enough safely concealed these items while displaying less valuable objects to fool any Germans who might raid their home.

The edicts continued. No Gentile could work for a Jew. No Gentile doctor could treat Jews, nor could a Jewish doctor treat Gentiles. Jews from all parts of Holland must relocate to Amsterdam. Jewish children could attend only Jewish schools.

And, perhaps worst of all, a Star of David must be worn on the outer garments of all Jews. The six-pointed star, made of yellow cloth outlined in black with the Dutch word *Jood* in the center, must be worn in plain view on the left breast, sewed firmly onto the clothing. This order must be complied with within three days, or face arrest.

All over Europe, thousands commiserated and empathized with the Jews over their new plight. King Christian X of Denmark demonstrated his solidarity with his Jewish subjects by wearing the mandated Star of David himself. A brave gesture, to be sure, but it could not save the victims.

Just as trees designated to be pulled up or chopped down have demarcations painted on their trunks, thus were the Jews identified. The prey was marked.

At least the Nazis got one thing right, Sofie thought as she sewed the yellow cloth star on Jan's coat, there's no better place for a *Magen David* than over a Jew's heart.

Mirjam ran into the house from school one day in late April, flushed and panting, her hair blown askew.

"What's wrong?" Sofie anxiously asked.

Mirjam gulped between breaths and tried to slow her gasps.

"Bloeme … didn't … show up … for school today," she said between breaths, "They said she got a notice to report for deportation to a labor camp!"

"Who said?"

"The teacher. She says Bloeme may never be coming back! Oh, Soof, I'm scared! Poor Bloeme; what will happen to her?"

Sofie stroked Mirjam's hair as she tried to calm her down. She, too, had heard of these deportation notices and knew that they were most often for older Jewish teenagers. Each morning she said a little prayer that the day's end would find her family intact.

The Germans had gradually, completely stripped away their rights. Sofie had seen many attempts by the Jews in Amsterdam and Maarssen to escape Nazi oppression. Some even married Gentiles, hoping to be shielded by virtue of their non-Jewish spouses. But these gestures proved futile. The Germans merely rounded up the unlucky Gentile brides and grooms and sent them to Mauthausen with a large letter "R" on their clothing for "race disgrace." Sofie began to fear seriously for the safety of her own family, but kept her feelings to herself. She knew she had to be strong for the girls' sake and not appear overly worried about their future, but she wondered at this new game the Germans were playing.

45

Sofie didn't know it, but the Germans were playing a carefully calculated game. Satisfied that they had curbed the Dutch resistance, they began the systematic round-up of Dutch Jews. They knew it must be accomplished in such a way as to invoke the least insurgence.

Knowing that all parents subconsciously prepare themselves for the day when their children grow up and leave home, the Germans reasoned that it would be easiest to round up teenagers and young adults first. After all, parents expect their teenage children to soon strike out on their own. If Jewish teenagers were deported first, their parents would be more likely to accept their departure than if the Germans tried to take young children or adult men away.

The S. S. left it to the Jewish Council to decide who would receive call-up notices and when. Soon, all the Rijnfeld girls had at least one friend who had received one of these notices. Sofie watched as saddened families of these young people waved goodbye from the trains bound for what they were told were work camps in eastern Europe.

She overheard fathers comforting tearful mothers by saying, "Now, dear, Dorotea will be just fine … she's old enough to take care of herself."

As angry as Sofie was at the members of the Council for their part in these scenarios, she also felt sorry for them. It must be a horrific responsibility to decide which families must send their children away to God knows what. She thanked God Jan had not been appointed to the Council. Families were torn asunder by these call-ups. No matter how mentally prepared a parent might be for a child to leave home, when the moment arrives it is wrenching. How must it feel to receive a letter that takes your 16 year old son or 18 year old daughter to a "work" camp in a foreign country?

Sofie learned the answer to that question sooner than she had dared think. It was a balmy afternoon with spring all around. The tiny, colorful growing things on the ground and in the trees were a sharp contrast to the austere military jeeps speeding along the streets and the ominous fighter planes droning loudly overhead.

Carla and Anneke were helping Sofie with supper in the kitchen. Elli sat in the living room with a book, while Jopie crocheted. Mirjam and Lena had turned a corner of the kitchen into a beauty salon, with Mirjam sitting erect on a chair while Lena wound sections of her little sister's hair onto cellulose curlers. Lena secured the last curler with a bobby pin, then draped a large triangular hair net over her work, wound the ends around the back of Mirjam's head and tied them together in front, above her forehead.

The house was quiet, with just the intermittent sounds of subdued conversation. The family's radio had been confiscated long ago. Still, it was a tranquil domestic scene, one that could almost make you believe there was no war, no Occupation, no Nazism.

Two brisk twirls of the doorbell sounded, piercing the quiet.

"I'll get it!" called Elli.

From the kitchen Sofie saw her jump from the sofa and run to the door. When she heard nothing, she called out, "Who is it, Elli?"

No response.

"Elli? Who was at the door?"

Elli appeared in the kitchen, very frightened. "It was a messenger boy in a German uniform. He said he came to deliver this." She held out a white envelope.

Sofie wiped her hands on her apron and took the envelope. Jopie had come in from the living room, and the sisters all gathered around their stepmother. Taking a hairpin from her hair, Sofie slit open the envelope and removed the folded paper inside. A large swastika was imprinted on top of the page. She quickly scanned the contents.

… hereby ordered to report … minimum of clothing and necessities … only one suitcase per person allowed …

"Soof? What is it?" Lena asked.

Sofie hastily composed her face into cheerful lines. "Nothing serious. Just another mandate to turn in all bicycles and radios. If the Germans kept better records, they'd know we turned in our radio months ago."

Jopie wasn't fooled. She came around to stand next to Sofie and laid a hand on her arm.

"It's a call-up notice, isn't it? The Germans are deporting us."

The sound of Jan's key in the front door rescued Sofie from having to answer. He entered and called out his customary greeting, "Man in the house!" He removed his hat and dropped it on the hall table. Loosening his tie as he walked toward the kitchen, he wondered at the silence that greeted him instead of the chorus of "Hi, Pappie" that always answered him. He saw Sofie and the girls standing in the middle of the kitchen, something like a telegram or a letter in Sofie's hand. He put his hands on his hips in mock indignation.

"Well, this is a fine how-do-you-do! I come home from a hard day at the salt mines, and this is the welcome I get?"

Sofie held the letter out. "You'd better look at this."

Jan's eyes skimmed over the typewritten words that would split his family apart. As soon as he saw the words *train station*, he knew. A knot the size of a grapefruit formed in the pit of his stomach as he read on.

> *Achtung!*
> *The following Jews are hereby ordered to report to the*
> *Amsterdam train depot at 7:00 a.m. on Tuesday, April 28, 1942*
> *for resettlement:*
> > *Jopie Rijnfeld*
> > *Carla Rijnfeld*
> > *Lena Rijnfeld*
> > *Ellinor Rijnfeld*
> > *Anne Rijnfeld*
> > *Mirjam Rijnfeld*
> *Only one suitcase per person will be allowed. No exceptions.*
> *Bring only a minimum of clothing and necessities, as you will be*
> *issued uniforms upon arrival at your ultimate labor assignment.*
> *Failure to comply with this directive will result in disciplinary action.*

Jan's hand fell limply to his side, still holding the letter. *Disciplinary action.* He knew what that meant.

He gestured toward the living room. "Come, girls, let's all sit down. I want to talk to you."

They all moved to the living room and sat down. The girls were silent, feeling certain of what their father was about to tell them, yet praying that somehow they were wrong.

Jan looked at his daughters, young women in the early bloom of life. His eyes filled with tears. He took a deep breath.

"Girls, this letter is from the Central Office for Jewish Emigration. It's an order to report ... the Germans want ... " He faltered, unsure how to break the news to his children.

Mirjam came to her father's rescue. "It's all right, Pappie. We know. The letter is our deportation notice."

Jan raised his head to look at Mirjam and tears ran freely down his cheeks. "Yes, *mammeleh*."

He crushed the letter into a tight ball in his hand. "Damn them! God damn them!" he spat. Sofie ran to put her arms around him.

"Pappie, don't," cried Lena, "We'll all be together. No one can take us away from you."

Jan raised his head to look at his daughter. Anguish welled up in him as he realized the misunderstanding.

Unable to tell Lena the truth, Jan broke free from Sofie's embrace and strode to the kitchen, cursing himself for the coward he was to break down like that.

Sofie watched him go, knowing what pain he must be suffering. It was up to her to make it easier for him.

She turned to face her stepdaughters. Should she sugar-coat it? No, she decided. Just speak the truth and get it over with. That's the best way.

"My dears, the call-up is just for you girls, not all of us," she said.

The girls sat dumbly in disbelief, even though in recent months they had seen this happen daily. Friends they had known all their lives were forced to leave their homes and families for an unknown fate. And as the news of each one had reached the ears of the Rijnfeld girls, their fear surfaced anew.

But they hadn't experienced the full measure of this fear until Soof told them it was now their turn. Strangely, none of the girls cried or displayed any fright But deep down, they knew what it meant to leave their parents and the security of their home at the whim of the Nazis.

And a terror such as they had never known gripped them in a relentless vise.

"Her children rise up and call her blessed, Her husband also, and he praiseth her..."

CHAPTER 4

THE SCENE AT THE TRAIN STATION was bedlam. From overcast skies fell a light mist that mixed with the acrid smell of the train's exhaust fumes. The platform was crowded with small groups of people everywhere, families bidding tearful farewells to loved ones about to depart. And overall was the ominous presence of the S. S. officers and soldiers stationed at strategic points throughout the platform. Sofie stood with her family amid the jostling crowds, hardly believing how radically their lives had changed since the arrival of the call-up notice for the girls just three days ago.

It was early this morning, before dawn, that Sofie had shocked the family with her announcement. Jan and the girls were already downstairs in the kitchen having a light breakfast. Nobody felt much like eating, but Jan had wisely insisted that they put something in their stomachs.

Sofie came down the stairs, carrying a small suitcase. She placed it with the six others lined up in the vestibule. She walked into the kitchen to find the girls sitting soberly around the table with Jan, who was staring into a cup of coffee long ago turned cold. The sight of their faces convinced Sofie even more firmly that she was making the right choice.

"Girls, I'm going with you," she declared.

Carla smiled wanly. "Thanks, Soof. We'd hoped you'd come see us off."

"No, dear, you don't understand. I'm going with you on the train."

Jan's head snapped up. "What are you talking about? You can't go with them; you weren't ordered to. The Germans won't allow it. Besides, who knows what —"

He stopped in mid-sentence and Sofie knew he had been about to say "who knows what will happen to you."

She said, "I know I wasn't ordered to. But we can't let the girls go off alone, to God knows where."

"Soof, if anyone should go with them, I should. They're my daughters."

"Our daughters. And you couldn't go with them, Jan. I hear they separate men and women. No, I'm going with them, and that's that. I've already packed, so I won't hear any arguments. Besides, we'll be late if we don't get going. Things will go much worse for us if we show up late," Sofie said.

Jan had never loved Sofie more than at that moment. He pulled her to him and held her tightly.

Sofie felt her heart constrict at the thought of leaving him. Had there been time to debate the issue, her resolve might easily have been weakened. Jan was unaware of the sleepless nights Sofie had spent wrestling with this decision, debating the consequences, questioning her true motive. After all, she didn't have to go, and nobody would fault her for staying.

Why, then, was she making this choice? Did she have a hero complex? Was she trying to prove herself to Jan? Or was she truly going for the girls' sakes and just having second thoughts as the hour of departure drew closer?

The girls sat still in their chairs, not quite believing what they had heard. Soof was willing to sacrifice her freedom, her new life with Pappie, to go with her stepdaughters to whatever fate the Germans handed them? Truly, they had been blessed to have such a stepmother.

Mirjam sat with her head bowed, feeling guilty at the sharp pang of relief she experienced at Soof's announcement. She should protest, convince Soof to stay safely behind. But in truth, she was terribly glad that Soof would be with them.

As she would later learn, her sisters all felt the same way.

And now here they were, saying good-bye to Pappie for what might be a very long time. After more hugs and kisses, Jan reluctantly took Jopie's arms from around his neck and held her hands in his. He looked at Soof and said, "You'd better queue up. That lieutenant over there keeps staring at us." He gestured toward the uniformed S. S. officer standing impatiently by the edge of the platform, glaring meaningfully at the Rijnfelds.

"Pappie, will you do something for me?" asked Jopie.

"Of course, *schatje*," Jan answered.

"Tell David that I love him, that I'll always love him. But if he gets tired of waiting for me … "

"Hush. I'll do no such thing. You can tell him yourself when you come back," choked Jan, "The war can't last much longer. You'll all be back before we know it."

Jopie began to weep. At this, the S. S. lieutenant lost patience. He strode over to the Rijnfelds and grabbed Jopie's shoulder, spinning her around to face the check-in queue. He angrily pointed toward it with his finger, shouting in German.

Sofie saw Jan's fists clench and his face redden in anger at the officer's treatment of his daughter. Fearful of what her husband might do and the repercussions that might ensue, she tugged at his arm and implored him to walk away.

The girls, all of them weeping now, followed Sofie and Jan toward the officer standing in the middle of the platform, holding a clipboard. They took their places at the end of the crawling queue, Jan inching his way forward with them as he stood to one side.

Finally, they stood before the check-in officer. The girls gathered around Sofie as close as they could, taking solace in her leadership.

This is it, Sofie thought. No turning back now. Her insides quaked and she fought down the urge to run. Mirjam slipped her hand into Sofie's and held it tight. The contact brought Sofie back to reality and calmed her rising panic. She was needed. She had to go.

The S. S. captain looked at the women clustered together and asked, "You are all one family?"

"Yes," Sofie answered clearly. She made a show of bravado for the girls' benefit, not to mention her own.

"Name?"

"Rijnfeld."

With typical Nazi efficiency, the captain ran his pencil down the neatly typewritten list on his clipboard. He came to the name Rijnfeld, emphasizing his find with a jab of the pencil. He looked up at the little group centered around Sofie and counted them. Frowning, he said, "I have only six Rijnfelds listed here."

"Yes, these are my daughters and I am going with them."

"What is your name?"

"Sofie Rijnfeld."

"You are not under transportation orders," said the captain curtly, "Go home."

"You don't understand," explained Sofie, "I want to go with my daughters."

"*Nein*. Only those on the list." He pointed at the girls and said, "You! Get on board." He then turned toward the next person in line, dismissing Sofie.

Suddenly angry at his rude demeanor, Sofie stepped in front of the captain as he turned away from her. Setting her lips in a determined line, she confronted him.

"If my girls are going on that train, then I am going with them."

The captain shrugged. "Have it your own way, *Frau*," he said. If you want to get on that train, by all means, go ahead."

Afraid he might change his mind again, Sofie quickly herded the girls away for one last farewell to Jan. Each of the girls hugged their father once more. Sofie refused to look at him, afraid she would lose her hard-won composure. She closed her eyes tightly and kissed him, hard.

"I'll take good care of them," she whispered in his ear.

She turned away with her eyes still closed and inched forward. Only when she was sure he was behind her did she open her eyes. She hoped the girls were following close behind, but she dared not turn around to make sure. If she turned to look back at Jan, she was sure she would run straight back into his arms and never leave them.

Without a backward glance, she boarded the train.

The boxcar was crowded, with nowhere to sit except what floor space could be claimed. There were no toilet facilities, save for a metal bucket which was soon filled to capacity. By midmorning Sofie felt a strong urge to urinate, but tried to put it out of her mind. She looked over at where Jopie and Carla stood leaning against the rough boards that made up the walls of the car. Carla kept shifting her weight from one leg to the other, trying to ignore the growing need to relieve herself. The other four girls were crouched in a dim corner of the car. Anneke's face was buried in her arms, and Sofie peered closer to see if she was crying. Anneke lifted her face and gave Sofie a wan smile, wrinkling her nose.

Sofie understood. Several of the younger children and the elderly on board had been unable to control their bladders. With no sufficient receptacle and no hope of a respite to use proper facilities, they had been forced to relieve themselves where they stood. In the poorly ventilated car, the smell was powerful, and the lurching of the train caused the small puddles of urine to run in rivulets from the back of the car where the embarrassed offenders had retreated as close to the bucket as possible to relieve themselves.

Those who were not too tired to stand relinquished their places on the floor of the car. The corner where the younger Rijnfeld girls sat was far enough away from the creeping puddles to remain dry, but it was nonetheless a repulsive situation. By the looks on their faces, Sofie knew her daughters were as uncomfortable as she was, and she was proud at how stoic and uncomplaining they were.

Lena stood up and stepped over her sisters' legs to move closer to her stepmother.

"Soof, where do you suppose we're going?" she asked, loudly enough to be heard above the noise of the churning train wheels.

"I'm not sure," Sofie answered, "I suspect we'll end up in some kind of work camp."

"What sort of work?"

"Something to aid the war effort, I imagine … the German war effort, that is."

A woman in her sixties with snarled grey hair stood near Sofie and Lena, listening to their hesitant conversation. Privacy in such close quarters was an impossibility. The train gave a lurch and the woman lost her balance, pitching forward into Sofie's arms.

"Sorry, dearie," she apologized.

"That's all right."

The pale, tired woman looked at Sofie knowingly. "I heard what you said to the girl. You oughtn't to put her off with stories about 'war work.' Why, she's a grown woman herself, old enough to handle the truth."

Perplexed and offended, Sofie answered, "I don't make a practice of lying to my daughters. If I knew for certain what the truth is, I would certainly tell them."

Lena heard the woman accuse her stepmother of keeping the truth from them. She put a protective hand on Sofie's shoulder in a gesture of solidarity.

The woman silently regarded them. "You really don't know, do you?"

"Know what?" asked Lena testily.

"Where this train is headed. We're going to Westerbork, the transit camp in Drente."

Sofie hadn't heard of Jews being sent to Westerbork.

"What will happen to us there?" she asked the woman.

"We get temporary work assignments until they ship us out east, to one of the camps in Poland or Germany or Czechoslovakia."

Lena gasped. Sofie glanced around and saw that the other girls, and indeed everyone else in the boxcar, were listening intently to this news.

"How can you know this for sure? We haven't heard any reports confirming this. We might just end up making uniforms for the army or rolling bandages or some such thing."

"Suit yourself, dearie. Some people find it easier to pretend rather than face reality. It helps them get through. If that's the way you want to play it, I won't try to tell you differently. But it's only going to be harder on you in the end."

The woman turned and stumbled over legs and bodies lying on the dirty wooden floor and walked toward the rear of the car, bracing her hand on the wall along the way to keep her balance.

Sofie's resolve to be strong for the girls was renewed at the strange woman's cavalier acceptance of their alleged fate. She motioned to her sad-eyed daughters crouching on the floor to stand up. As they slowly found their balance on stiff limbs, she gathered as many of them into her embrace as she could fit. Reaching out a hand toward Jopie and Carla, who stood on the outskirts of the huddle, she reassuringly squeezed each of their hands in turn.

"We'll get through this, girls. Nothing can break us as long as we have each other."

By nightfall, the train had slowed into the little town of Drente in northeastern Holland. Westerbork had been built by the Dutch government before the Nazi invasion as a refugee camp for Jews who had crossed the border illegally to escape persecution in Germany. Once the Nazis dominated Holland, they took over Westerbork for their own purposes and used the German Jewish refugees to maintain efficiency and order in the camp.

Utter fatigue had drawn Sofie into a fitful doze when she was awakened by the lurch of the train screeching to a halt. There was a roar as the train's heavy door slid open on its track. The brightly lit station caused the exhausted passengers to squint at the sudden glare. Fortunately, Sofie and the girls had been sitting near the door, so they were not separated in the crush of people clamoring to disembark from the stuffy, malodorous boxcar.

As they moved away from the tangle of people tumbling out of the train cars, Sofie noticed S. S. guards with saber-tipped rifles standing at virtually the same locations on the platform as had the guards at the Amsterdam station. Except there were no German officers to round up bewildered passengers and direct them to the appropriate place. Instead, men and women dressed in civilian clothes bearing the yellow cloth star with the word *Jood* standing out plainly in the center were directing the flow of traffic toward a row of makeshift tables at the far end of the platform. Long lines formed in front of each table.

Sofie gave a deep sigh. Everything these days involved waiting in long lines. She was tired, grubby, and in desperate need of a toilet. Beyond the check-in tables, she saw a Jewish man and woman directing new arrivals toward the latrines. She hoped she could hold out that long.

Sofie peered around the heads of the women in front of her to see what was taking place. Each new arrival removed her jewelry and handed it over to the person checking her in. Sofie took a quick mental inventory: pearl earrings, the delicate gold wristwatch Jan had given her for on their second wedding anniversary, and her wedding ring. She was thankful that she had long ago removed her diamond engagement ring and deposited it safely at her parents' home in Maarssen. After the incident at Nazi Headquarters in Amsterdam when their car had been blatantly stolen, Sofie had wisely hidden her ring. Its monetary value might well be something they would need to fall back on after the war. She stubbornly held onto her wedding ring, though. It had never left her finger since the day Jan put it there, and she wasn't about to take it off now.

As her turn in line approached, Sofie churned with the quick decision she must make. The earrings she disqualified immediately. It would be too obvious if she tried to remove them now. She fingered her wedding ring, desperately wanting to slip it off her finger and hide it in her brassiere. The plain gold band wasn't worth much more than fifty guilders, even on the black market, but its sentimental value was priceless. She couldn't just docilely hand it over for the Germans to melt down.

But, her practical side argued, if she was going to try to keep a piece of jewelry, wouldn't it be more sensible to keep something of real value, something that might help them in the uncertain days ahead?

All this went through Sofie's mind in the space of an instant. She continued to peer around the heads of the women in front of her as if she were tired of standing in line — which she didn't have to pretend — while she surreptitiously opened the clasp of the gold watch on her left wrist. Shaking her hand slightly, she let it fall into her cupped palm, catching it in the fold of skin between the base of her thumb and forefinger.

She grimaced and rolled her head from side to side in an exaggerated advertisement of a stiff neck. She brought her left hand to the back of her neck and massaged the muscles, letting the watch fall from her hand. She bent her head down to widen the aperture between her neck and her collar, praying the watch wouldn't miss its mark and fall on the ground. She felt the coolness of the metal sliding down her back and catch on the back of her brassiere.

Now she worried that there might be a telltale bulge in the back of her dress, and she casually turned her back away from the woman behind her, pretending to survey her surroundings. Only two more women to go before it was her turn …

The lines moved steadily, and when Sofie approached the table and was instructed to relinquish her jewelry, she quietly sucked in her breath. She removed her earrings, but hesitated as she pulled off her wedding ring, pleading with the man behind the table to let her keep it. Not surprisingly, her request was denied. When at last she was dismissed, Sofie eased out her breath in relief. She had succeeded in keeping the watch, another small victory.

That ordeal over, Sofie's attention turned once more to her full-to-bursting bladder. She and the girls grabbed their valises under their arms and dashed toward the women's latrine, only to be met by another queue. Elli sobbed in frustration and pain, having spent the entire day uncomfortably full. When their turns came, they gave no thought to the primitive wooden bench with multiple crude openings cut in the middle, nor to the complete lack of privacy and dignity. Their only concern was to rid themselves of the painful pressure.

The new arrivals went through their in-processing in a methodical daze. They were assigned barracks and given a meal of thin cabbage soup and bread-and-butter sandwiches. There was also watery coffee, but it was hot and tasted heavenly to Sofie.

They soon found themselves ensconced in Barrack B, a dormitory-style structure with fifty cots lined up in tight rows. Each cot had a thin pad for a mattress and a thin blanket of a scratchy material. There were no sheets or pillows. As far as the exhausted women were concerned, they would have gladly collapsed to sleep on the wooden planks of the floor.

Sofie shivered under the thin blanket, the night air here chillier than in Amsterdam. She peered through the darkness at the girls asleep on their cots next to hers. Their exhaustion had enabled them to fall asleep immediately, for which Sofie was grateful. She, however, found herself unable to sleep, despite the day's ordeal. Her wristwatch was now tucked inside her underpants, the safest place she could think of. She thought about Jan, wondering what he was doing tonight, alone in their house. She knew he must be beside himself with worry. She would find out tomorrow if and when she could write to him.

As she lay there, Sofie repeated her vow to Jan.

"I'll look after them," she whispered into the darkness, "I promise you, Jan. I promise."

Dear God, she prayed, help me get through this. Help me to be strong for the girls. Help me bring all of us safely home to Jan.

From across the room she heard someone muttering softly in a kind of sing-song. She sat up and looked around to see who else was awake. In the shadowy darkness she saw a figure standing next to an empty cot, bobbing her upper torso forward in short, choppy movements.

"Shema Yisrael, Adonai elohenu, Adonai echad … "

The voice was familiar — Sofie looked closer and recognized the brusque, grey-haired woman from the train. She was *davening*.

Sofie lay back down and echoed the woman's prayer in a whisper. Funny, she thought, I've never really considered myself a religious person, but I've prayed more in the past twelve hours than I have in my whole life.

And in fact, she felt a sense of strength when she prayed, a comforting feeling that she wasn't left alone to deal with this incredulous turn of events.

The grey-haired woman finished her prayer with a long, intoned "Amen."

"Amen," Sofie whispered. She closed her eyes and slept.

*"She seeketh wool and flax,
and worketh willingly
with her hands."*

CHAPTER 5

MAY 29, 1942

My darling Jan,

   This is the first time they have allowed us to write to our families, but I am grateful that we are allowed to write at all. Let me assure you that the girls are well and handling things beautifully. You would be so proud of them, Jan. I know I am.

   Daily life is not as terrible here as I feared during the long nightmare of a train ride. We have sufficient food and make do with the extra clothing they distributed to us. The girls and I are housed in a large barrack with 43 others, including this one strange woman we met on the train. Her name is Esther and she is convinced that we are all doomed to be deported to a concentration camp in the east. It's hard to keep a stiff upper lip in the face of such pessimism. Yet Esther prays every night, after everyone else is asleep. I can't figure her out, but I'm not sure I want to try.

   I had hoped that the girls and I would all get the same work assignment, but they have split us up. Anneke, Lena and I are assigned to the sewing shop. I almost laughed when I heard where they were placing me, but I thought better of it. I soon found out that if you don't know how to do something, you learn how — fast. So now I am a seamstress. After the war I might even put my new skills to good use! Do you think there will be many vacancies for a Dutch woman who makes German army uniforms?

Mirjam, Elli, and Carla are working in the battery factory. They disassemble used batteries to be recycled into new ones. It seems many of the women and children are assigned this job. Their hands are smaller and can reach into tighter places than a man's hands. It's messy work and the battery acid takes its toll on their skin, but one of the women in our barrack has some cocoa butter she keeps hidden from the guards, and it helps the irritation.

Jopie works in the kitchen. At first I worried about her being separated from us during the day, but we see her at every meal. She says she doesn't mind too much, and she's even able to sneak some extra rations once in a while.

The whistle has just blown for evening roll call, darling, so I must close now. I pray God you are safe and well. Don't worry about us, Jan. We'll be fine. Just keep the home fires burning and pray that the war ends soon. The girls send you their love and will write you soon. Take very special care of yourself, my dear husband.

> *Always,*
> *Soof*

p.s. Jopie says to be sure and give her love to David and to tell him she will write to him as soon as she can.

Sofie folded the letter and sealed the envelope to mail after roll call. They had been at Westerbork for over a month before they had been allowed to write home. Sofie was anxious to write to Jan and reassure him that life here was not as horrible as they feared. She had tried to sound cheerful and upbeat for Jan by interjecting a bit of levity in the hope that this first letter would ease his mind somewhat.

While they lived spartanly and followed a fairly strict regime, there was no starvation or mistreatment. The camp administration even urged the inmates to devise ways to entertain themselves, and encouraged the weekly cabarets staged by the prisoners in the large camp hall. Often the Germans themselves attended, laughing and applauding as if they were at the Folies Bergere. Many prisoners were accomplished musicians, and as the Germans enjoyed fine music, they secured the prisoners' respective instruments and encouraged concerts, even making requests. One of the women in Sofie's barrack had been trained for the opera, and occasionally she performed arias from well known operas, accompanied by the camp "orchestra." The Germans seemed partial to Wagner and often requested to hear his works. This upset the more Orthodox Jews in the camp, who disapproved of celebrating the music of so vehement an anti-Semite, no matter how legendary and gifted.

The scope of talent ran the gamut from children who recited poetry to a young couple who waltzed like professionals. Besides being entertaining in themselves, the shows served to keep up morale. Neither Sofie nor the girls ever participated, however. As Carla put it, why should they parade themselves for the amusement of the Germans in the audience? Sofie agreed, but she privately thought the cabarets were effective in distracting the inmates from more unpleasant matters, like the fact that they were imprisoned in a German-run transit camp for no reason beyond the fact that they were Jewish.

Another surprise to Sofie was that the Germans' presence in the camp was not as evident as she would have thought. The day-to-day running of Westerbork was left to the Jews themselves. A group called the Order-Service had been formed, much like the Jewish Council in Amsterdam, which maintained basic discipline and order in the camp. The members of the Order-Service were only too glad to be on the council, as they enjoyed special privileges denied to the rest of the prisoners.

Not surprisingly, this fostered resentment and jealousy among the inmates. Not only were the *kapos*, as the Order-Service members were called, unpopular for the duties they performed, but they were regarded by the rest of the camp as traitors who kowtowed to the Germans to their own selfish ends. The Germans delighted in the hatred and discord sown throughout the camp, knowing from the beginning that the establishment of the Order-Service would lead to such strife. They took perverse pleasure in the animosity that festered from this internal hierarchy, laughing at the Jews who could not even get along with their own.

Another weekly ritual took place at Westerbork, one that was certainly distracting but not at all entertaining. Each Monday night, a list was posted in the mess hall with the names of a thousand inmates slated for deportation on the transport that left every Tuesday for "the East." Sofie had come to learn that "the East" was a catch-all term for the more notorious concentration camps in eastern Europe: Auschwitz, Bergen-Belsen, Sobibor … Most of the transports were bound for Auschwitz in Poland, a destination dreaded by the Westerbork population. Even though the Germans referred to deportation to the Polish death camp as a "labor assignment," the Jews knew better. No one ever returned from Auschwitz. Sofie remembered the first time she and her daughters had seen the list …

They had just finished the evening meal, and the more observant Jews were reciting in rapid Hebrew the blessing after the meal. Sofie turned as she heard derisive laughter from the back of the vast hall. Two S. S. guards stood against the wall, pointing at the praying prisoners and laughing at their rocking motions as they *benched*.

Her attention was diverted by an S. S. sergeant who entered the hall carrying a sheet of paper and a small hammer. He placed the paper at eye level on the wall and fastened it to the rough board with a sharp rap of the hammer. This done, he ambled over to where the other two guards stood, greeting them in a cheerful voice. Taking a toothpick from his pocket, he casually leaned against the back wall and picked his teeth while he and his comrades watched the scene that ensued.

In one movement, everyone who had been sitting on the hard benches at the long wooden tables rose and dashed over to where the paper was nailed. Those seated closest to it got there first, but others pushed and shoved, trying to get a closer look. Sofie rose from her bench in apprehension, puzzled as to what was happening. She saw some people shout in joy after reading the notice on the wall, hugging whoever happened to be next to them. She saw some emerge from the throng with heads hanging low, women weeping, comforting arms around friends shoulders.

Instructing her daughters to stay where they were, Sofie approached the diminishing crowd huddled around the notice. She stood on tiptoes trying to read it, peering around the heads blocking her view. Finally able to squeeze her way up front, she saw a typewritten list of names with the next day's date as a heading.

"What is this?" she asked a short man standing next to her.

He looked quizzically at Sofie. "You must be new here. It's the weekly deportation list."

"Oh, a roster of our permanent labor assignments?"

The man snorted. "Call it what you like, *Mevrouw*, but it all means the same thing. If your name's on this list, you're on your way to Auschwitz." He looked again at the list. "My name's not on it. But I'm hoping it will be next time."

"You want to be sent east?" Sofie asked.

"*Mevrouw*, we're all going to be sent somewhere. Most of the transports go to Auschwitz, but once in a while they go to Bergen-Belsen in Germany. The word is that next week's transport is bound for Belsen."

"And Belsen is better than Auschwitz?"

The man was surprised at Sofie's naiveté. Patiently, he explained that Bergen-Belsen had originally been designed as a transit camp for Jews they planned to exchange for German prisoners held in territories not under Nazi control. Belsen was sometimes referred to as the *Austauschlager* or "exchange camp." A Jew sent there always had the hope of being exchanged for a German prisoner and sent to Palestine.

Sofie listened intently to this information. She had a lot to learn.

"If you're wise, *Mevrouw*," her teacher continued, "You'll keep your eyes and ears open and listen to what goes on around here. There are many tricks to be learned in the game of survival. And it's one game we can't afford to lose."

On the walk back to the barracks, Sofie explained the procedure to the girls.

" ... so we'll have to be sure to check every Monday to see if we're on it," she explained. "Maybe we'll get a chance to be exchanged at Bergen-Belsen. If we can get to Palestine, we can send for your father."

Listening carefully to their stepmother, the girls didn't notice the S.S. guard who had fallen into step behind them, one of the pair who had laughed at the Jewish prisoners saying grace after the meal. Sofie and the girls were the last to leave the mess hall, since everyone else had quickly departed after checking the deportation list. By this time, the Rijnfeld women were so accustomed to the ubiquitous guards that they paid no attention to the one who loitered by the door, smoking a cigarette. He watched as they passed by, his eyes lingering on Lena. He took a last drag on the cigarette and flicked it to the ground, grinding it out with his boot. Hitching up his rifle strap more securely over his shoulder, he pushed back his cap and followed the women as they made their way toward the barracks.

Quickening his step, he overtook Lena. He caught her arm and said, "What's the hurry, *liebchen*?"

Lena yanked her arm free and resumed walking. In one swift movement the guard shoved his hand under her skirt and grabbed a handful of her backside. She shrieked, causing her sisters and Sofie turned around. Lena's chest heaved with indignation, and she pressed her hands down the sides of her skirt to prevent further intrusion.

The guard stood there, laughing. Without thinking of the possible consequences, Sofie marched up to him until she stood face to face.

"What do you think you're doing?" she spat angrily.

"I do anything I please," the guard laughed. "Is this your daughter?" He ran a finger around Lena's ear while she grimaced and strained away. "She's quite a looker, even if she is a Jew."

Sofie's hazel eyes flashed her rage. "You keep your filthy hands off her and the rest of my family. I don't want to see you come near us."

The guard quit laughing. Savagely, he backhanded Sofie across the mouth, knocking her to the ground. The girls cried out and rushed to kneel by her prone body. A sinister smile spread across the guard's face. He sauntered past the girls gathered around their stepmother, and gave Lena a lascivious whack on the bottom. She straightened abruptly and whirled to face her tormentor. His smile turned rakish. He chucked Lena under the chin and said, "We'll meet again, *liebchen*."

Lena smacked his hand away and turned back to her dazed stepmother. She heard his receding laughter as he walked away, and she shuddered at the implication of his words.

The girls helped Sofie to her feet and brushed the dirt from her dress. The sleeve had ripped and the skin underneath was red and scraped. Her split lip was bleeding profusely and her cheek was already starting to swell.

"Oh, Soof, I'm so sorry. This is my fault," cried Lena.

Sofie started to shake her head no, but pain stabbed through her. Unable to speak just yet, she looked at Lena with sorrowful eyes and touched her arm: you didn't do anything wrong.

Jopie understood and sudden tears blurred her vision. Her stepmother's love and concern for them all never failed to fill her with emotion.

"Soof, you can't confront the Nazis that way," she chided. "We're not free anymore. They can kill us if they want to."

The other girls chimed in their agreement. Reluctantly, Sofie admitted to herself that they were right. The old rules no longer applied. This was a whole new game, like her mess hall teacher had instructed her. If she wanted to survive, if she wanted to protect the girls, she had to learn to play by the Germans' rules. It was a bitter pill to swallow, but for the time being she had no other choice. With the girls' help, she struggled to her feet and limped back to Barrack B, humbled for the moment but not defeated.

The guard strolled back to his own quarters well pleased with himself. He had been itching to get at that pretty Jew girl for weeks now, but hadn't been able to until his commanding officer left for Berlin on leave. He had given his men strict orders against consorting with the Jews, no matter how enticing. He saw his opportunity tonight to check out the situation, to see if this one would give him any trouble. Now he knew he could have her anytime he wanted. He'd have to be discreet, of course. But she wouldn't fight him now, not after the smack he'd given her cow of a mother.

He smiled at the memory of how easily Sofie went down when he backhanded her. His commanding officer also disliked physical abuse of prisoners, so this chance to knock some respect into these Jew bastards was an added bonus.

Twenty-five year old Klaus was a prime specimen of Nazi manpower, the pride of the *Führer's* armies. Six feet tall with blond hair and blue eyes the color of cornflowers, he was the epitome of a model Aryan. During his youth in Frankfurt, he had never known any Jews personally, though he was aware that Frankfurt had a large complement of them. They were respected physicians, prominent lawyers, esteemed university professors, successful businessmen. Why, Klaus' family doctor was a Jew. Old Dr. Königsberg had taken care of them for as long as he could remember. He had even cured Klaus' mother of a severe case of whooping cough when the family thought she would have to be hospitalized. Klaus was aware that many of his parents' friends didn't like Jews, but he was too busy with school and soccer to wonder why. As a teenager, Klaus didn't particularly dislike Jews nor did he like them. They just didn't affect him one way or the other.

When Klaus was fifteen, Adolf Hitler was elected Chancellor of Germany. Klaus stood in the crowd of onlookers that were lined five-deep along Frankfurt's main boulevard to watch Germany's new leader pass by in a victory motorcade. He watched Hitler wave and smile to the cheering men and admiring women. Young children were held up over their parents' heads to get a glimpse of the *Führer*.

Klaus watched transfixed as a goose-stepping army unit marched past, their smart uniforms bearing the insignia of the Nazi party on white armbands. He raised his eyes to the flagpole on the main square and the large red flag undulating in the stiff breeze, emblazoned with a giant black swastika. A sense of pride began to form inside Klaus, a feeling of strength, of power. He was part of the Fatherland's promising future, and he had an inkling that exciting times lay ahead for him and for Germany.

The next day, Klaus joined the Hitler Youth Organization.

That summer, Klaus and the 500 other boys and girls who comprised the special camp for Hitler Youth learned how to become productive Aryans who would serve the Reich and help Germany take its place as the head of the supreme race on earth. Youngsters ranging from ages 10 to 18 spent six weeks at these summer sessions, engaging in rigorous daily sports activities and paramilitary exercises. The goal of Hitler Youth was strength through physical fitness and mental discipline. When Klaus was not performing calisthenics with his fellow campers in the vast athletic field, he was learning to march in a straight line. He also perfected the straight-armed Nazi salute, smartly snapping his right arm straight out in front of him with fingers together and thumb bent at a slight angle, his heels clicking together in a divinely loud clap.

There were classroom lessons, too, where the boys learned various means of identifying the Jewish enemy. There was, of course, the large hooked nose that made the Jew look as devious as he was, and the shape of his head. A caliper was sometimes used to measure the heads of suspected Jews, as it was well known that they lacked the perfect formation of the Aryan head. The dark coloring of a Jew was also a telltale sign. Granted, there were some dedicated Nazis who had dark hair, but those undesirable genes would be diluted in subsequent generations until they were no more. When Klaus was called upon by the instructor to stand before the class as an example of Aryan features in their purest form, it was the proudest moment of his life.

The girls at Youth Camp had their classes, too. Outdoor physical training was encouraged for them as well, but it focused more on stamina and grace rather than strength. Their routines with large hoops and balls were so expertly choreographed that they were often commanded to perform at Nazi rallies. The girls practiced for hours, hoping that one day they might show off their skills to the *Führer* himself.

Classroom instruction for the girls consisted of much the same material as for the boys. They were shown drawings and photographs of the evil Jew, the better to identify him and turn him in to the appropriate authorities. They were instructed to be wary at all times, as Jews were known to prey upon innocent German girls and do unspeakable things to them. The girls' eyes were like saucers as they listened to the instructor enumerate the horrific deeds decent Aryan girls have suffered at the hands of Jewish vermin.

Most importantly, though, the girls learned how they could best serve the Reich and further the Nazi cause. It was imperative, the instructor admonished, for every Aryan girl age 16 and above to bear a child for the *Führer.* Not only would this produce the next generation of Hitler's armies, but it would expedite the purification of the Aryan race.

To this end, the boys and girls at Hitler Youth Camps were brought together socially, under strict supervision, where those of acceptable age could meet and hopefully spark an alliance that would ultimately result in a pregnancy. There was no shame in such pregnancies, despite the youth and unmarried status of the girls. Indeed, parents of daughters who bore children for the *Führer* boasted to their friends of the accomplishment, as did the parents of sons who sired the next generation of Aryans. Between the ages of 17 and 20, Klaus fathered four children. It was a most pleasurable obligation that he was more than happy to fulfill.

By the time Klaus was 21, he was an experienced soldier in Hitler's army. While most of his comrades had obtained commissions as officers, Klaus preferred to remain in the enlisted ranks where he felt he could best serve the Reich's needs. He had requested a transfer to a tank battalion, eager to participate in the planned invasion of Poland. His request was granted, and Klaus felt a heady sense of power and superiority as he stood tall and proud on the hatch of his tank as it rolled triumphantly through the streets of Warsaw. The *Führer* was right: they were indeed the Master Race.

Klaus remained in Warsaw until 1941 when he was transferred to Westerbork Transit Camp in the Netherlands. Holland had been conquered the year before, and although deportation of Jews had not yet been fully implemented, it was ordered that the camp be made ready to receive deportees on short notice.

Klaus was pleased with his new billet, his self-confidence and acknowledgment of his own superiority in high gear. He was only too happy to show these Jews what true Aryan power was. There were not many Jews interned at Westerbork his first year there, so Klaus concentrated on absorbing every aspect of camp operation. He compared notes with his comrades and learned that those who had not attended Nazi-run camps or schools lacked his thorough education on the evils of Jewry. Many times when Klaus and another soldier had the evening watch, he passed the slow hours by enlightening his companion on the treacherous ways in which Jews had stabbed Germany in the back.

Yes, Jews were the lowest of vermin; they were not even people. Klaus knew this well, which is why he was angry with himself for finding Lena Rijnfeld so attractive. A Jewish slut was fine for a toss, if one was not too particular and careful not to incur the wrath of his superiors. But this Lena was damn beautiful, a woman who would have been worthy of his most zealous attentions had she been Aryan. Funny, she didn't particularly look like a Jew, with her fair coloring and delicate features …

Klaus shook his head to chase away the ghost of Lena's image. He refused to allow himself to feel such humanly natural desire for someone so subhuman as a Jew. But desire was undeniably there, which made Klaus clench his fists in anger. He'd show that Jew bitch what she was really good for …

70

*"Strength and dignity
are her clothing, and she
laugheth at the time to come."*

CHAPTER 6

JOPIE OVERTURNED AN EMPTY BUCKET and sat down for a moment to rest in the steamy camp kitchen. She took from her apron pocket an envelope addressed to her and hastened to open it. It was from her father, and she hoped he would have some word of David. She hadn't heard from her fiancé for some time and it worried her. Her chapped fingers, cracked and irritated from constant dishwashing in the harsh industrial soap used in the camp, smarted when she ran them under the envelope flap, but she paid no attention. They were in better shape than those of her sisters working in the battery factory. The battery acid ate into their tender flesh, leaving their hands raw and blistered.

Eagerly, Jopie opened the letter and smiled at the familiar handwriting. Her father began by telling her that David was fine; he was just getting over a bout of measles that had laid him low for a while. She was not to worry that she hadn't heard from him; he would write to her just as soon as he regained some of his strength.

... and don't think for a minute, Jopie, that David is not going to wait for you. He's told me a dozen times since you left that you are never far from

his thoughts. I've no doubt that he wants nothing more than to carry out the wedding plans you two made before the war broke out. And I intend to escort you down that aisle, with Soof on your other side!

Sweetheart, please give your sisters my best love and tell them I will write to them soon. I plan to write to each of you individually, but you must know that no matter who gets the letter, the love inside it goes to all of you ...

Jopie finished the rest of the letter, noting the message her father requested she pass on to Soof, from her parents. All was well with them. They were still in Maarssen and relatively unaffected by the German occupation. Jews were somewhat safer in the countryside and the Mecklenbergs had not been subjected to the same calibre of Nazi edicts that had devastated Amsterdam.

Jopie bit her lip, reminding herself that when she wrote back to her father she mustn't mention the incident with the Nazi guard. He was already terribly worried about their situation and Jopie didn't want to add to his anguish.

She folded the letter back in the envelope and placed it inside the waistband of her skirt. She had fashioned a crude satchel from a piece of torn apron and saved all her letters from home in it, safely hidden under the mattress of her cot. Often, before lights-out, she took one of the precious letters, either from her father or from David, and read it over and over, trying to lose herself in the memory of how life used to be.

Although she had only been at Westerbork a few months, the memory of her comfortable life in Amsterdam was rapidly fading, becoming more like a distant recollection than a tangible reality of the recent past. This frightened her. She didn't want Westerbork to become her normalcy. She didn't want to get used to waking before dawn each day to face the steam kettles in the camp kitchen that turned her face a bright red. She dreaded that it might become second nature to lower her eyes whenever she passed a German guard or S. S. officer. To look them in the eye would be taken as defiance, or at the very least bring unwanted attention. Every day she made a point of telling herself that this was not real life; this was a temporary situation that she must endure for a time. One day the war would end and she would have her life back. She had to believe that. She had to.

But every day it became harder and harder to convince herself, for real life had been reduced to the stifling humidity of a kitchen and endless tubs of hot dishwater. She looked down at her hands, her red, chapped hands with the broken nails and ragged cuticles that often bled. She laughed ruefully to herself as she remembered that these were the same hands she had proudly held up to her friends and family to display her new engagement ring. Her skin had been white and smooth then, the diamond sparkling against a border of red-polished fingernails. Where was her ring now, she wondered. Was some German woman wearing it? Or had it been sold to buy needed items for the German army? Her ring had been confiscated when she first arrived at the camp. Remembering what had happened to Soof when she had confronted a guard, Jopie was glad she hadn't protested, but she fervently wished she had taken her stepmother's advice and hidden her ring at the Mecklenbergs' house for safekeeping. It was odd, she mused, that she wasn't sure what upset her the most: the condition of her hands or the loss of her engagement ring … Once more in the barracks, Jopie folded her father's letter and hastily slipped it underneath her mattress, after first glancing around to make sure there were no watchful eyes to discover her hiding place. The huge factory whistle sounded afternoon roll call, and Jopie hurried out to join her family in the routine line-up. She didn't notice how automatic her response was to the blast of the whistle, with barely a second thought to what she was doing and why.

Another Monday night arrived. As usual, the evening meal was quiet as the prisoners wondered whose names would be on tonight's list. Sofie shifted her weight on the wooden bench, trying to find a more comfortable spot on the unyielding seat, which she concluded was impossible. She glanced at Mirjam, who sat across from her, and gave her a smile. Mirjam attempted a half-smile in return, her lips tight. She had barely touched her food, which worried Sofie. They all needed to keep up their strength.

At last the door opened and a private entered with the usual hammer, nail, and single sheet of paper. He held the hammer under his arm while he positioned the paper on the wall, holding the nail at the top. A loud rap, and the entire mess hall converged on the list even before the guard could walk away. Annoyed, he pushed at the men and women who crowded toward him in their efforts to read the list. When this yielded no results, he raised his pistol above his head and fired one shot into the air. The crowd stilled and slowly retreated a safe distance from the guard. There was no sound now but the ping of the empty bullet casing as it fell to the floor on the other side of the hall. His way now cleared, the guard left the mess hall, muttering in German as he went.

The prisoners had been collectively holding their breath when the gun fired. They now released it in one great sigh of relief. Anneke and Sofie, who had instinctively grabbed onto each other when the shot was fired, still had their arms around each other. They relaxed and Sofie patted Anneke on the back reassuringly. They strained to see the list, but on the outskirts of the throng they couldn't make out the names.

Anneke spotted Elli close enough to the list to read it, and called to her to check for their names. Elli edged nearer to the wall where the list was posted, wiggling her way through the elbows and shoulders that surrounded her until she was right in front. She ran her finger down the page until she came to the Rs. Sofie held her breath again as she watched Elli scan for their names. She had never revealed to the girls or Jan her fear that they would be transported to different camps. If some of the girls were separated … she shuddered, knowing that another moment of reckoning was seconds away.

Elli fought her way through the crowd to the back where Sofie and her sisters stood.

"We're on it, we're on tomorrow's transport," she said, smiling happily.

"All of us?" Anneke asked.

"All of us!"

None of the sisters questioned why Elli seemed so happy to find their names on the deportation list. Sofie's relief was so great she almost sagged to the ground. The girls all started talking at once, asking Sofie questions and speculating about their destination. In the midst of the hubbub it dawned on Sofie that Elli had been as delighted to find their names on the transport list as if they had just been invited to dine with Queen Wilhelmina. She must have been as worried as Sofie that they would be separated, transported at different times to different destinations.

Sofie couldn't decide which was worse: the loneliness of unspoken fears or the despair of shared ones …

As the Rijnfeld women made their way to Barrack B, Sofie only half-listened to the girls talking among themselves. She knew that it was more important now than ever to take her wristwatch with her and keep the Germans from getting their hands on it. Eighteen-karat gold, with a diamond chip on the number 12, it would be worth a fair amount of money if she needed it. What for, she didn't exactly know, but instinct told her that life as they knew it was about to take a turn for the worse, and she would need all the resources she could muster.

But where to hide it? Certainly not in the one suitcase each person was allowed to bring on the transport. Her dress pockets wouldn't do. What about the spy novels she had read where people smuggled jewels in their mouths? No, she could hardly act nonchalant with a wristwatch in her mouth! She managed a wry smile at the thought.

An idea came to her, but it was so bizarre she was reluctant to let it form completely in her mind. Still, desperate situations call for desperate measures. If she could only get up the courage …

"Soof, what's on your mind? I could practically see the wheels turning, you were thinking so hard," Carla said.

"I, uh, — I was thinking of the fun we all had that day at the lake a few summers ago. Remember? It was right after Pappie and I got married … "

" … and we took a picnic and spent all day there!" Lena chimed in, "I had a such a great time that day."

"You mean you had a great time showing off in that two-piece bathing suit," teased Jopie.

"Yeah, Pappie had a fit when he saw her in that!" Carla added.

"That's why I didn't let him see it until we got there!" Lena explained mischievously.

They all laughed, and Sofie congratulated herself for having diverted the girls attention so neatly. She hadn't told any of them about her watch, not because she didn't trust them, but because she intuited that too much knowledge could be a dangerous thing. Better that they didn't know. It was her responsibility.

In the barracks, those who were on the list for deportation were scurrying about, packing their meager belongings and exchanging farewells and mementos. Sofie saw Esther press some photographs into the hand of another woman who was staying behind, imploring her to keep them for her. One was a portrait of what Sofie guessed to be Esther's parents and siblings. Another worn photo, dog-eared at the edges and slightly torn in the middle, was of a young woman holding a swaddled baby in her arms. The third photograph showed a smiling bride and groom on their wedding day. Esther?

Sofie couldn't imagine the gruff, scraggly woman who shared her quarters as a glowing young bride or a proud new mother. Maybe the pictures were of someone else ...

Sofie listened as Esther gave instructions to the photographs' new guardian. The address of her nephew in America was written on the back, she explained. If Esther didn't survive the war and come back to claim these pictures, would she please send them to her nephew?

Sofie turned back to her own packing. The girls were in good spirits, considering. She heard the loud clang of the huge camp generator that simultaneously turned out all the lights in the barracks, after which time no prisoner was allowed out on the grounds. The building went dark and a groan of protest rose from the women who had not finished their preparations for tomorrow's journey. Some continued to work in the dark as best they could; others gave up and lay down on their cots. What they did not finish packing must be left behind, as there would be no time in the morning to complete the job.

From the row of cots behind her, Sofie heard someone get up. She raised up on an elbow to see who it was.

"Lena!" she whispered, "Where are you going?"

"To the latrine."

"Why didn't you go before lights-out?"

"I didn't leave myself enough time. I'll just sneak out there very quickly and slip right back," Lena whispered.

"Can't you wait until morning?"

"No. I guess it's nerves," Lena replied.

Sofie's instinct was to persuade Lena not to take such a chance, but she hesitated. The odds of Lena getting caught outside after lights-out were slim; the few guards on duty at night stayed close to the camp's perimeter. And even if she did get caught, what could they do to her now? They were all heading east in the morning.

Sofie whispered a last caution to Lena to be quick and careful. Lena promised she would, and crept lightly along the wooden floor, avoiding the creaky places as best she could. She continued along the wall until she came to the door. Opening it the tiniest crack, she peered out. Seeing nothing, she opened it a tad more.

Nothing.

She slipped out the door and crouched down. Another glance around and over her shoulder.

Nobody had spotted her. Good. Now she just had to get to the latrine behind the barracks and back again.

Anxious to have it done with, she ran in a crouch as fast as the awkward position would allow. She hugged the side of the building and rounded the corner. Feeling more sheltered in the shadowy area between the two buildings, she straightened upright. Pleased with her success, she darted into the latrine.

She finished quickly and peered around the wall surrounding the latrine. Still deserted. She stepped out into the alley and glanced around. Her luck was holding.

Suddenly, she heard laughter and voices coming from the direction behind the latrine. Should she hide, or was there time to make it to the barracks before they rounded the corner? She bent her head, broke into a run, and collided full-length into Klaus.

Catching her by the arms, he smiled in pleased surprise. "What's the hurry, *liebchen*?"

Only too aware of the threadbare nightgown she was wearing, Lena struggled against his grip.

"I ... uh ... beg your pardon," she stammered, her face turned away and eyes downcast.

To her surprise, Klaus immediately released her arms. She crossed them in front of her in an instinctive attempt to maintain her modesty. Klaus stepped back and folded his arms as if waiting for something.

"What are you doing here after lights out?" he demanded.

"I — I had to go to the latrine."

"So? There's a bucket in your barracks."

Lena lifted her chin. "I am not an animal. As long as there is a way for me to maintain some semblance of dignity in this place, I intend to use it."

Klaus bristled at her sudden defiance. He glared at Lena for a long moment.

"You know I can report you for this," he said.

"I know."

"'Sir'. 'I know it, sir!'" he barked, "You Jews need to learn respect."

Lena said nothing.

"But," Klaus continued softly as he approached her, "I don't have to report you. Maybe you and I can become friends, eh, *liebchen?*"

He ran a finger up her bare arm, catching it in the shoulder of her nightgown. He tore it down in one swift movement.

Knowing better than to scream, Lena yanked herself away from his grip. Klaus grabbed her and shoved her roughly to the ground. He grabbed her throat with one hand and held her fast there. She pulled frantically at the hand, unable to move the fingers that squeezed her throat like an iron collar.

"Now see here, bitch, we can play it one of two ways. Either you behave like a good little girl, or I'll have you removed from tomorrow's transport list. You can stay behind and keep me company while your sisters and mother go on to Auschwitz."

Auschwitz. Suddenly the meaning of the word hit home, and for a moment Lena forgot her immediate predicament. They were going to Poland. So much for Soof's dream of being sent to Bergen-Belsen and possibly being exchanged to for political prisoners in Palestine …

Klaus increased the pressure on her throat, bringing her sharply back to the present. She choked and coughed.

"Well, *liebchen?* What's it going to be?" His hand released her throat and slid down to her breast, squeezing it cruelly through the thin material of her frayed nightgown.

Lena squeezed her eyes shut, unable to stop the hot tears that pooled in her eyes. There was really nothing to think about. She let her hands drop to her sides, where they hit the hard ground and lay limp, palms up. She didn't care what happened to her anymore.

Klaus leered in his triumph. He dragged Lena by one arm behind the latrine, the sharp stones on the cold ground lacerating her legs. Weak sobs escaped her lips as Klaus rapidly removed his jacket and unbuckled his belt.

Lena endured repeated onslaughts before Klaus dragged her back to Barrack B and dumped her unceremoniously inside the door. This, of course, woke the other occupants who stared dazedly at Lena's dirty and bruised body lying crumpled on the floor. Rape was not uncommon in transit camps like Westerbork, where the prisoners were still in good health and physically appealing. Their more unfortunate counterparts in the concentration camps were not subjected so much to this particular horror. Starvation and disease soon rendered them undesirable to even the most insatiable of German appetites. Lena would later wonder if rape wasn't the lesser of the evils.

Jopie was the first to recognize the crumpled form by the door. She flew out of her cot to Lena's side, calling for Soof. Darkness cloaked the cuts and bruises covering Lena's body, but Jopie could tell something dreadful had happened to her sister.

As gently as possible, Soof and Jopie lifted a dazed and silent Lena to her feet. It was impossible for Sofie to evaluate her condition in the dark. All she could do was put the poor girl to bed and wait until morning. She hoped Lena would be able to withstand tomorrow's journey in such condition.

The burden of responsibility pressed down upon Sofie with added intensity. Helpless to do much for Lena, she felt overwhelmed and inadequate. Sofie now realized what she had gotten herself into by coming with the girls. All of a sudden, her noble gesture seemed nothing more than high drama.

Guilt descended, swift and overpowering. She should never have allowed Lena to sneak out to the latrine. If she was going to be the brave protector, she would have to do better than this.

Sofie set her mouth in determined lines. Starting tomorrow, she would live the role she'd taken on, and stop play-acting. The part was proving more demanding than she'd bargained for. There was to be no rehearsal, and she'd better have the role down cold ...

*"She girdth her loins
with strength,
and maketh strong her arms."*

CHAPTER 7

THE SUN WAS JUST CLEARING the eastern horizon,
but Sofie and her daughters had been standing on the train platform
for over an hour. The Order Service arranged the scheduled Tuesday
deportees into three rows and they stood now in perfect alignment, just
as the camp *kommandant* demanded. The train that would take them to
Auschwitz was behind schedule, but the *kommandant* refused to let them
sit or otherwise relax their positions on the platform. The train's delayed
arrival annoyed him, and he vented his ire on the deportees, forcing
them to remain standing in strict formation, men on one side, women
and children on the other.

They had been fed only a lukewarm gruel earlier that morning,
and loud rumblings emanated from the stomachs of several women.
Mirjam couldn't suppress a snicker and succeeded in attracting the
attention of the *kommandant's* aide, a major who had been pacing the
platform for the past ten minutes, slapping the riding crop he carried
against his thigh. He paused occasionally to peer down the track for any
sign of the approaching train. Seeing nothing, he angrily smacked the
riding crop into his palm.

At the sound of Mirjam's giggle, he whirled to face the group of women who stared straight ahead. He slapped the crop against his thigh and shouted, "Silence! No talking!"

He continued to stare at the prisoners for a few seconds to lend impetus to his warning. Mirjam's cheeks turned red and her heart pounded in fear that she would be singled out as the culprit. The major's steely eyes seemed to bore into hers and she fought hard to keep from trembling. Droplets of perspiration dotted her upper lip.

Just when she felt sure her flushed cheeks and nervous demeanor would betray her, a loud blast from the train's whistle pierced the silence. Turning toward the tracks, the major saw a distant puff of smoke from the approaching train. He made a sweeping gesture with the riding crop to his subordinates and barked orders in German.

Mirjam quietly exhaled in relief. The train's arrival spared her from the major's wrath and brought an end to their agonizing wait on the platform. Some of the women had begun to sway in their places from standing at attention for so long. Fainting from exhaustion was no doubt an infraction with unpleasant consequences, so the train's arrival was indeed fortuitous.

Alongside Mirjam stood Elli, her face turned upward toward the warming sun. Eyes closed, she breathed deeply of the June air not yet polluted by the thick white smoke billowing out of the locomotive. She tried to mentally distance herself from time and place, pretending she was at home relaxing with a book in the back courtyard on a late spring day, the sun warm on her face and arms. She tried to drink in the beauty of nature she still believed in, to absorb as much sun and fresh air as she could hold before boarding the stifling train. A dreamy smile came to her lips and without thinking she began to hum softly to herself. It was a tune that Mammie used to sing to her when she was little, one she hadn't thought of in years.

Carla looked over at her sister and gave her a sharp nudge in the ribs with her elbow.

"Shush, Elli, you'll get us all in trouble," she hissed.

Startled out of her reverie, Elli looked around as if she'd quite forgotten where she was. Her pleasant imaginings had worked too well; she hadn't realized she was humming out loud. Returning her gaze straight ahead, she whispered out of the side of her mouth, "This is probably the last time we'll see the sun and breathe fresh air for God knows how long. I want to enjoy it while I can."

In answer, Carla gave Elli's hand an empathetic squeeze. Elli squeezed back and held onto her sister's hand. Carla followed Elli's glance and looked over to where their stepmother stood. Sofie was squirming slightly and her face wore an uncomfortable grimace. Next to her stood Lena, whose hair hung limply over a large, purplish bruise on her cheek. Jopie and Anneke stood wearily on her other side, and smiled encouragingly back at Carla.

Loud shouts brought the sisters' attention back to the train that squealed to a stop in front of the platform. The long train consisted of about twenty boxcars, each with a sliding wooden door that locked into place with a great iron bolt. Cattle cars. A tiny rectangular window high in the car's corner was the only opening, no more than twelve inches long and six inches wide, with thin iron bars across.

Members of the Order-Service approached each car and threw open the huge bolts. The doors slid back, revealing a dim inner vastness with bits of hay strewn on the floors. The S. S. guards began shouting at the exhausted and bewildered deportees, beckoning them to board.

"*Schnell! Schnell!*"

They shoved the prisoners toward the cars, pushing them into the gloomy interiors, continuing to push even when a car seemed filled to capacity. In the chaos, Sofie lost sight of Elli, Carla, and Mirjam. Lena was in front of her and Sofie grabbed the back of her dress as they were herded into a car that was already packed tightly with women and children. Instinctively, Jopie and Anneke did the same: Anneke taking hold of Sofie's dress, and Jopie grasping Anneke's. A sad caravan.

Sofie had no chance to locate her other three daughters, but prayed they hadn't been separated from one other in the crush. She sucked in her breath and squeezed as far back as she could against the sweating bodies already in the car, motioning to Jopie, Lena and Anneke to do likewise, lest they be caught in the wooden door as it was slid back into place, shutting out all but the merest light that peeped in through the small window. The iron bolt fell into place with a loud clang.

One hundred and fifty people were loaded onto each boxcar which, under reasonable circumstances, could accommodate twenty. There was no room to sit or lie down. They were packed so tightly that the shorter women and younger children found breathing difficult. The suitcases they were permitted to bring were loaded into the last two boxcars. Luggage would be redistributed upon arrival, they were told.

Once the train had been loaded and the German officials had departed the platform, the other inmates crept out to wave and bid farewell to their fellow prisoners. "Goodbye! Goodbye! God bless!" And more faintly, "*Shema yisrael, Adonai elohenu, Adonai echad ...* "

After a stifling eternity, the train gave a great lurch and slowly chugged away from the station with its pitiful cargo. It gradually picked up speed, white smoke blowing out in rapid puffs. When it was no longer in sight, those left behind reported to their work stations.

Sofie and her daughters lost track of time as they traveled on the train that surely must be taking them to hell. They had no idea how long the journey to Auschwitz would be, but even five minutes in the overcrowded, suffocating boxcar seemed almost unbearable. How would they sleep, Sofie wondered, with no room to move? When it became apparent that they would be traveling throughout the night, Sofie observed some of the passengers sleeping where they stood, relying on those crammed in around them to brace them upright.

Others fell down purposely, thinking to clear a space on the floor. This tactic succeeded only in angering the others and rewarding the perpetrators with caustic reprimands and, occasionally, a few well-placed kicks. It frightened Sofie considerably to see these women — some of whom she had come to know at Westerbork as kind and cheerful — reduced to physical blows over what amounted to a few inches of space on a hay-strewn wooden floor.

The air in the boxcar became intolerably stuffy, and the glassy-eyed travelers looked longingly at the tiny rectangle located high in an upper corner. Placing it thus allowed enough ventilation to forestall complete suffocation, while preventing the inhabitants from reaching the window and viewing their surroundings, calling out to townspeople, or just breathing fresh air. Since the train passed through populated areas, it was essential that the prisoners not be allowed to communicate with private citizens, and the Nazis made sure this was impossible.

Sofie didn't know which repulsed her more: the fetid air or the lack of proper toilet facilities. Only one small tin bucket had been placed in the rear of each car for elimination. One bucket for 150 people on a journey that would last many days.

Far worse than the indignity was the fact that the bucket became full long before nightfall of the first day. The contents of the filled-to-the-brim receptacle sloshed over the sides with every sway of the train, splashing those who stood nearest. The stench permeated the stagnant air, causing everyone to cough and retch.

There was very little conversation. Those who had not fallen into a dazed stupor from lack of food, water, and air prayed softly to themselves. When the faint light from the window heralded the dawning of their second day in transit, everyone finally accepted that they would not be stopping for food and drink.

Worse than cattle, Sofie thought. Even livestock being transported to slaughter are fed and watered.

Slaughter. The thought hadn't occurred to Sofie before, but now she considered the possibility. Perhaps they weren't being taken to a labor assignment at all. Perhaps they were being denied food and water because they were only going to be killed anyway. A coldness formed in the pit of her empty stomach, temporarily chasing away the hunger pangs. She looked around to see if she could spot Jopie and Anneke beyond the miasmic figures plastered against her. Unable to see either one of them, she spoke their names.

"Jopie. Anneke."

No response save for a loud cough. She called louder.

"Jopie! Anneke!"

An arm reached up above the tangle of bodies, like a periscope breaking the surface. Leaning over as far as she could, Sofie grabbed the outstretched hand and clasped it tightly. She was unable to tell whose hand she held, but the connection calmed her, dissolving the cold knot in her stomach.

The indignant people underneath the bridge formed by the clasped hands broke them apart, reclaiming what little space had been theirs. Sofie's fear and loneliness escalated. She tried to calm down by reminding herself that this hellish journey must end sometime. And if she was this frightened, how must her daughters be feeling?

Sofie knew she had to summon a courage she never believed she possessed in order to be strong for the girls. They looked to her for their fortitude and she mustn't disappoint them ... or Jan. The family depended on her. If they put on a bold face to these Nazis and showed them their mettle, surely things would turn out all right.

It was perversely fortunate that none of the train's occupants knew that this hellish journey was far better than the reality awaiting them at the other end ...

Seemingly light years away, a pale and thin Jan Rijnfeld opened a letter he had just taken from his mailbox. He recognized Sofie's script on the envelope and stood looking at it, trying to connect the familiar handwriting with the woman who had brightened his life for too short a time.

Strange, he didn't rush to tear open the envelope as he always had when a letter came from Sofie or the one of the girls. He sensed that this letter brought news he didn't want to know, and his fingers shook when he tore open the flap. The letter began as it always did, with Soof assuring him that she and the girls were well. Jan offered up a quick prayer of thanks. He read on.

> ... *our last night at Westerbork. Tomorrow we are being deported to a labor camp in Poland. I pray this letter reaches you, as I'm not sure if I will be able to write to you again. Try not to worry, darling. Thank God we are all going together, and I will take care of the girls. They are strong young women, Jan. You would be so proud of them ...*

Jan sat down heavily in an armchair. He couldn't finish reading the letter. Though Sofie hadn't said so, he was certain his family were being sent to Auschwitz. He crumpled the letter in his hand and tried to choke back the response that came over him. He squeezed the letter tightly in his fist and leaned his forehead against it, sobbing unashamedly. He was torn with conflicting emotions. He wept for the fate of his family — his flesh and blood, and the new love he had been blessed with. He berated himself for allowing Soof to go along with his daughters and subject herself to a fate she might have avoided. At the same time, he felt humble and grateful that his daughters had been blessed with a stepmother who would risk her own life to safeguard theirs.

Jan quieted. He sat slumped in the chair, legs apart, his hands upturned and limp on his lap. He looked anew at the letter still crumpled in his hand. Slowly he unfolded it and smoothed out the creases. His red-rimmed eyes scanned the last brief paragraph. It revealed Soof's typically optimistic attitude.

Unreasonably, he felt a sudden anger toward her. How could she so easily continue to believe that all would turn out to the good? Why wasn't she miserable and stricken, as he was? At least Soof had the girls with her. Jan didn't even have the solace of his wife's comfort or his daughters' presence.

He smoothed the page once more before rising to place the letter in the drawer of the roll-top desk, on top of a pile of all the other letters he had saved from Soof and the girls. He felt ashamed at his irrational resentment. While he sat in his comfortable house with conveniences he took for granted, he berated Sofie's optimism in the face of true hardship. He realized that basic creature comforts would now seem like luxuries to his wife and daughters. In his guilt, he wished the Nazis would take him away, too. At least he would suffer the same fate as his family and not languish in comforts they were deprived of.

He heard Sofie's voice, then, talking to him as clearly as if she were right beside him, appealing to his sense of logic. What good would it do to have the Nazis take you away too, her calm voice said. There's no point in the whole family being torn apart. Better you should keep the home fires burning until the war is over, Jan. Once Hitler is defeated, we'll be coming home to you.

Jan resolved that if Soof could stay strong, so would he. The sense of guilt clung tenaciously, and it would take some time and effort to shake it off. It wasn't palatable to his male ego to admit his wife had taken on a responsibility that by rights belonged to the head of the household. But there was no room for guilt or self-pity in his resolve to be as optimistic and forbearing as his wife, nor would he allow himself to become mired in depression. Though he couldn't be with his family, he could provide moral support, albeit in absentia. Soof's optimism was contagious, and Jan intended to spread it as far and wide as possible. His spirits lifted at the implication of his new role in his family's survival. The Rijnfelds were a force to be reckoned with, and at this moment, Jan felt ready to take on Hitler himself.

"She is not afraid of the snow for her household; For all her household are clothed with scarlet"

CHAPTER 8

A GRATING SQUEAL OF METAL on metal pierced Sofie's ears. The train was slowing, slowing, until it came to a jolting halt that pitched its tightly packed passengers forward, then abruptly backward. The Rijnfeld women and the other prisoners were so crammed together that their reaction to the jolt was little more than a slight, collective sway.

They had been traveling for three days, though the passage of time ceased to have meaning for the pitiful lot inside the boxcars. Only by the narrow streak of pale light that came through the tiny barred window could they tell day from night. Dark clouds covered the gray sky, depriving them even of the beacon of hope the sun's rays might have brought as it shone through the bars.

The stench inside the car was far worse than anyone could have imagined. It bothered Sofie considerably that she personally contributed to the putrid odor. Her pants were sticky and heavy with excrement, the latrine bucket being far too remote for her to have made use of it. Had she reached it, she would have only succeeded in splashing fetid waste on those standing or kneeling nearest to the bucket, and their retaliations were not pleasant.

Sofie witnessed such a scene hours before. An unfortunate man standing immediately next to the bucket was soiled yet again by someone relieving himself into the overflowing receptacle.

"See how you like it!" he screeched, and violently flung a clump of feces into the face of the perpetrator.

There was a scuffle and cursing as the infuriated man was upbraided by his neighbors, while others restrained the victim when he would have fought back.

What's happening to everyone, Sofie fretted. Will we all become like that?

Such instances were rare, though, as most people chose to retain what dignity they had left and resist capitulating to the decline that had overtaken this poor soul. But trapped with him as they were, no one wanted to exacerbate the situation by challenging him.

There was a far more important reason why Soof had not attempted to use the bucket. Before boarding the train at Westerbork, Sofie had stolen a moment alone in the barracks and retrieved her small gold watch from its hiding place. She rolled the watch into as much of a ball as the soft metal links would allow, and quickly pushed it up her anus as far as it would go. She allowed herself a grimace at the discomfort caused by the unavoidable haste and lack of lubricant.

When she was reasonably certain that the watch would not expel itself, she stood up beside her cot and straightened her skirt. Her heart was beating fast. She felt an odd sense of detachment at what she had just done. It was as if she was standing to one side, watching someone else perform this distasteful chore.

Sofie put a trembling hand to her face and wiped away beads of sweat from her brow and upper lip. She knew that if she pondered a moment longer on what circumstances had forced her to do, she would succumb to the panic that threatened to engulf her. She took several deep breaths, refusing to yield to the hysteria rising in her throat. How could she have resorted to such an act?

You do what you need to do, an inner voice answered. You do what you must to ensure survival.

As Sofie stood in the stinking cattle car, she felt reassured by the now-familiar discomfort in her rectum. The watch had not been expelled; it was yet safe where surely no one would think of searching. There might just come a time when its value would come in handy as collateral.

"*Raus, Juden! Raus!*"

Bright light blinded the prisoners crowded in the car as its heavy doors were thrown open. Loud voices were shouting at them, beating them with sticks. Doberman pinschers and German shepherd dogs were barking furiously, straining at the harnesses held by brown-shirted S. S. guards.

"*Raus, raus*! Get out of the cars!"

The frightened passengers stumbled out of the cars, some literally falling out onto the platform. Sofie blinked against the unaccustomed brightness and anxiously looked around for her daughters. They emerged from the train wide-eyed and pale. Carla's beautiful brown curls now lay plastered to her face and neck, dark with sweat. Sofie waved and the girls ran toward her. Their collective embrace formed a little group unto itself which attracted the attention of the ubiquitous S. S. The guard standing closest to the Rijnfelds blew his whistle at a nearby *kapo*. The prisoner wore a striped camp uniform, but he appeared to be healthy and self-assured. He didn't walk around in fear, eyes downcast, shoulders slumped.

At the guard's signal, the *kapo* raised high a knobby stick and brought it down hard on the tightly-clenched huddle. It fell first on Elli's back and she screamed in surprise and pain. Before any of them knew what was happening, another blow struck, this time on Anneke.

Sofie instinctively covered her head with her arms. The S. S. guard signaled to the *kapo* to desist and gestured to a line of new arrivals forming on the platform. The *kapo* shoved the frightened women in that direction, Elli and Anneke whimpering in pain.

It was then that Sofie noticed the yellow star on the *kapo's* shirtfront. Their tormentor was a Jew. A fellow Jew was beating them, serving the Nazis?

It was incomprehensible.

Jopie spoke first. "Please, *mynheer*, can you tell us where are we going?"

The *kapo* indicated several huge chimneys rising high above the platform only a short distance away. "You see that? You arrive by train, but that's how you're going to leave here," he sneered, pointing to the acrid smoke billowing out of the chimneys.

91

Unfortunately, he spoke loud enough for the S. S. guard to overhear. He strode quickly over to the *kapo*, and shoved him mightily in the chest. The *kapo* stumbled backward and fell onto the wooden platform, no longer confident. The guard bellowed something in German and yanked him up by his collar. The S. S. had a strict rule against providing newly arrived prisoners with any information that might cause panic. Punishment for breaking this regulation was death. Whimpering and pleading for mercy, the *kapo* was dragged off to a nearby hut.

Soon, the *kapo's* screams and moans could be heard from inside. A second *kapo* approached Sofie and the stunned girls and pushed them back in line. The doomed *kapo's* screams grew fainter until they stopped completely. The girls glanced surreptitiously over their shoulders to see the S. S. dragging him out of the hut, his face a bloody pulp. He was dumped unceremoniously into a wheelbarrow and taken quickly away by yet another *kapo*.

At that moment, Sofie realized that all the mores and values of her upbringing were no longer of any importance. At Auschwitz, there was a new set of values to live by, and if she did not learn it quickly, she and the girls would not last long.

They won't get me, Sofie thought fiercely. I don't want to die, and I will get out of here.

"She perceiveth that her merchandise is good; Her lamp goeth not out by night."

CHAPTER 9

KONZENTRATIONSLAGER AUSCHWITZ lay in a swampy valley in southwestern Poland, about an hour outside of Krakow. It was a remote corner of the country that most Poles considered quite inhospitable. In summer, the camp sweltered in the hot, breezeless air. In winter, it was beset with snow and ice storms that swept in from the Vistula River.

In short, it was the perfect place to establish the Reich's largest extermination center, part of Himmler's "Final Solution to the Jewish Question."

Auschwitz was the German name for the Polish industrial town and railroad junction *Oswiecim*. It bore the distinction of becoming the first Nazi concentration camp instituted in occupied Poland. As early as 1940, an S. S. delegation was sent to Oswiecim to investigate a set of barracks that had been constructed on the outskirts of the town during World War I. Between the First and Second World Wars, the barracks had been used by the Polish military to house troops.

The initial investigation denounced the suitability of Auschwitz as a *Konzentrationslager*, but a subsequent inspection determined that, with some construction work, the camp would serve their needs. Necessities such as watch towers, barbed wire and electrified fencing were added. When top Hitler aide Rudolf Höss conducted a final inspection in April of 1940, all proved satisfactory. On June 14, 1940, KL (for *konzentrationslager*) Auschwitz was officially opened with Rudolf Höss as *kommandantur.*

In the early years of the war, Auschwitz was intended to serve as a concentration camp for Polish political prisoners and other criminals. Only after 1942, when the "Final Solution" was implemented, did Auschwitz became the Reich's primary killing center for Jews and other undesirables. Its vast size — the camp stretched for miles — was surely an important factor, as tens of thousands of Jews and Gypsies were exterminated daily towards the end of the war. Moreover, the sub-camp system within Auschwitz provided slave labor for the factories, fields, and quarries that contributed to the German war effort.

It was also the Nazis' intention to reap the economic benefits of mass extermination. With all manner of goods in short supply, the Germans saw to it that nothing from the victims was wasted. Hair shorn from arriving Jewish prisoners was sold to German firms at a price of fifteen pfennigs per kilo, and was then woven into cloth. Lampshades were manufactured out of Jewish skin that had been easily removed from the skeletal corpses on which it hung loosely. Soap was made with body fat of Jews, though starvation made this key ingredient scarce. Rare bars of the soap were prized by German women and often presented as hostess gifts at social occasions by generous officers' wives who took smug pride at obtaining such a treasure.

For the military personnel assigned to Auschwitz, life was pleasant and orderly. Every facet of normal life was replicated for the staff. The expanse of the camp afforded personnel their own theater, soccer stadium, swimming pool, and symphony orchestra. High-ranking S.S. officers and their families lived in spacious homes flanked by lush gardens. Even traffic regulations were imposed and enforced. But how does one reconcile every-day comforts with the living hell they were provided to facilitate?

The complete chaos that reigned on the ramp as the trainload of Jews disembarked was organized into the two large groupings of men and women. The queue in which Sofie and her daughters inched along was more of a column of people than a line. A separate column of men, about eight across, stretched alongside for hundreds of meters. There was no more shouting; only low murmurs could be heard, and even those were silenced by a few terse words from one of the S. S. guards.

The June air was thick with fear and train smoke. With her peripheral vision, Sofie tried to observe the other women in line. Most were young, in their late teens or early twenties. Many had babies and young children. Sofie noticed one young woman heavy with child. She looked exhausted and pale, and Sofie's heart went out to her. The train journey had been horrible enough; Sofie couldn't imagine the added discomforts of advanced pregnancy.

They took several more steps forward as the line progressed. Their belongings, they had been told, would be retrieved later. For now, hand luggage carried by the arrivals was collected by *kapos* and other prisoners on work detail. A grizzled little man in his prison uniform of striped trousers, shirt, and tam snatched a lady's handbag and then a younger girl's rucksack. The Rijnfelds watched his dead eyes as he went about his business. He kept his head down for the most part, avoiding the faces of those in line. He shuffled past Sofie, hesitated the briefest moment, then shuffled backwards with surprising agility until he was at Sofie's side.

"Try for the right," he muttered, and then he was gone.

"What? I didn't — "

"No talking!" a guard ordered.

Sofie obeyed immediately, focusing straight ahead and hoping the guard would move on.

Elli, standing next to her, whispered, "What did he say to you?"

Sofie spoke out of the corner of her mouth. "He came and went so fast, I'm not sure. I think he said, 'Try for the right.'"

"What does that mean?" Elli asked.

"I don't know. Hush, here comes the guard."

The guard worked his way up the line, searching for the source of a loud wailing. He homed in on a young woman with a squalling infant in her arms. She was trying vainly to quiet the baby, and doubled her efforts when she saw the guard bearing down on them. She looked up hesitantly at him as he stopped beside her, expecting a harsh reprimand. Instead, he smiled indulgently.

"I'm sorry," apologized the young mother, "He's cutting some teeth."

"I understand, *Frau*. These things sometimes happen," he said calmly.

The woman smiled in visible relief at his sympathy.

Abruptly, the guard snatched the baby from his mother's arms. Holding him by his legs, he swung the infant wide into a low brick wall where his soft skull smashed like an overripe melon.

The baby's mother began screaming like a madwoman. The guard promptly removed his sidearm and fired one shot. She fell immediately.

Only a few feet away, the Rijnfeld girls clutched one another in mute horror. The episode had lasted no more than two minutes, but to the shocked witnesses, the motions were slow and surreal.

Lena doubled over and retched. Sofie tried to calm her, afraid of attracting more undue attention. But the guard was walking away, calling nonchalantly over his shoulder to another prisoner to clean up "that" from the wall.

Sofie gathered Lena in her arms and crooned softly to her, trying to distract her from the grisly scene. The other girls tried to distract themselves, as well, from the incomprehensible sight.

The line continued to move forward until Sofie and the girls stood facing an S. S. officer with fair hair, cold blue eyes, and a gap between his upper two front teeth. He cut an impressive figure in a snug green uniform complete with shiny black boots, white gloves, and a polished cane. Like so many of the German military men, he held a cigarette between his fingers and puffed frequently. With a sure eye, he surveyed the closely huddled Rijnfeld sisters and gestured with his cane to the right. When Sofie also turned to the right, the cane came down in front of her to block her passage.

"How old are you, Mother?" he asked in a curiously gentle voice.

Sofie met the steely eyes unwaveringly. "Forty-three."

The officer regarded her another moment, then lowered the cane. "Right," he said, dismissing her.

The girls breathed an audible sigh when their stepmother rejoined them. As they tailed the line of women who had already been directed towards the right, they could hear the officer's appraisal of the next prisoners.

"Left," he said, pointing to a six-year-old girl. To the girl's mother he said, "You, to the right."

"Please, sir, may I not go with my daughter?"

The officer smiled. "Surely, madam. Go right along."

The rest of the induction procedure took place so hurriedly that Sofie was unable to keep the girls together or stay with them. There was no loitering allowed; as soon as a prisoner finished at one of the five stations, she was sent on to the next. Failure to move quickly enough resulted in a sharp prod from a rifle, or a crude shove.

The first order of business was to have the women strip naked, despite the presence of male S. S. guards. This was a favorite practice of the Nazis. There was degradation in nakedness, and vulnerability. For the Orthodox Jewish women, to whom modesty at all times was a requisite, this humiliation carried an even greater weight.

When all their clothes had been taken away, the new arrivals had their heads shaved, as well as their body hair. The mounds of shorn hair were removed and taken to a storage building where it would be sold to make woven cloth and pillow stuffing.

The naked, bald women were prodded to the next station for showers, delousing, and disinfection. The announcement of the word shower caused some of the women to gasp in fear, but Sofie didn't know why. Personally, she welcomed the chance to wash. They were pushed into a large room fitted with shower heads in the ceiling. Many of the women embraced and wept. Others began to pray. The tension permeating the room was palpable.

After a few agonizing minutes, the nozzles were activated and cold water rained over the women. Cries of relief and joy washed over them along with the icy water. To Sofie, it was all very puzzling.

Station Three was for registration of personal effects. Once again, Sofie stood in line and waited her turn, knowing her most important possession was still safely hidden. She was grateful that the girls were somewhere ahead of her, for she didn't want her secret revealed to them. The less incriminating information they had, the safer they would be. As for her other personal effects, well … material goods were of little importance now.

There were two more women in line ahead of Sofie. The first one declared that she had no personal items; everything had been taken at the railroad platform. The work-detail prisoner, a Pole, told the woman to turn around and bend over. She complied. The Pole inspected the woman's vagina and rectum for hidden money or jewels, causing Sofie's eyes to widen in panic. She couldn't be found out now, not when she was so close to successfully smuggling in her wristwatch!

Sweat prickled her freshly shaven armpits as the woman in front of her submitted to the same inspection. What was she going to do when they discover the watch? What will happen to the girls?

Sofie was jolted out of her thoughts when the Pole barked at her to step up to the table.

"Turn in all valuables and money." The Pole sounded like an automaton.

"I — I have none," Sofie stammered. The Pole stood up and moved to the side of the table for yet another orifice inspection.

"Bend over," she commanded.

Sofie closed her eyes and turned around. It's all over, she thought.

A scream from Station One tore through the building. S. S. guards ran towards that sector. A young woman of no more than 22 was screaming and clutching the sanitary belt she wore. A *kapo* darted around her flailing hands, trying to tear off the narrow belt. Workers from all stations went running to the scene.

Sofie wasted no time. She quietly sidestepped her way to Station Four, praying that when the chaos subsided, the Pole would forget that she hadn't inspected Sofie. She waited in line to be issued her prison uniform, trying to look like nothing was wrong. Inside, she felt like screaming, too.

After interminable minutes, the Pole returned to Station Three and resumed her duties. She seemed to have forgotten Sofie, who didn't dare look back. The line seemed to crawl, but finally she was issued a grey dress of a thin, rough material with two yellow triangles sewn on the front in the shape of the Star of David.

She had made it.

Sofie would learn later that the triangles of various colors sewn to prison uniforms denoted the status of the prisoner. Political prisoners bore red triangles; professional criminals, green; "asocials," such as Gypsies and prostitutes, black; Jehovah's Witnesses, violet; and homosexuals, pink. Most uniforms were fashioned of material with broad vertical stripes. In the unlikely event that a prisoner attempted to escape and actually made it outside the camp, the highly visible uniform would facilitate his capture.

The final station of in-processing was where new arrivals had their prisoner identification numbers tattooed on their forearms. Hygiene was not a priority, and the same needle was used repeatedly with no cleaning. Many prisoners ended up with severe infections. As she waited in yet another line, Sofie saw a chance at last to retrieve her smuggled watch. The close call at Station Three had badly shaken her, and she now wanted to unburden herself, as much of the stress of hiding the watch as of the watch itself.

The line snaked along the wall. Sofie pressed her back as close to it as she could without attracting attention. She made a show of scratching her neck, her arms, her thigh, as if she had lice or some other irksome skin irritation. As naturally as possible, she made as if to scratch her bottom. She was grateful at that moment for the lack of undergarments. She reached under the rough material of her dress and probed her rectum while simultaneously contracting. To her great relief, she felt her fingers touch the metal links and she pulled out the watch.

One more prisoner to be tattooed before it was her turn. Her luck held. Fortunately, the other women in line were too immersed in their own situations to be concerned with Sofie's activities. She cupped the watch in her palm and surreptitiously wiped it on the skirt of her dress to remove as much waste from it as possible. Her head snapped up when she heard an angry voice barking at her in Polish. Sofie assumed it was an order to step up to the table, so she complied.

The tattooist was a prisoner herself, incarcerated for the crime of theft. By cooperating with the Nazis she earned herself a habitable existence. She was a stout, blowsy woman with three large moles on her face. It appeared she enjoyed her work. She had no use for Jews, and found great satisfaction in jabbing the tattoo needle into their skin. Sometimes she would surreptitiously spit on the unsterilized needle for good measure.

Sofie sat down on the stool in front of the small wooden table. The woman grabbed her arm roughly and slammed it flat on the table, palm up.

"Wait," Sofie said, "I have something to show you."

She brought her other hand with the watch clutched in it up on the table and turned her cupped palm up slightly, enough to give the Polish woman a good look at the watch.

The woman's eyes narrowed. The gold of the watch was no longer shiny, but there was no mistaking its quality.

Sofie spoke quietly. "Make my tattoo small, and the watch is yours."

She's an odd one, the woman thought. "What do you care what size it is? It won't matter in the long run."

"It matters to me. When I get out of here, a small tattoo will be easier to remove."

The woman snorted. "The way you'll be leaving here, you won't need to worry about such things.

Sofie didn't reply. Both women were silent as each contemplated the possible consequences of the transaction. If the Pole reported the attempted bribe to the Nazis, Sofie would surely be killed immediately. If the woman accepted the bribe but was caught, she too faced death. It was a risk for both women, though clearly more so for Sofie. The woman could easily take the watch and do as she pleased.

The Pole wondered why, after successfully smuggling in her watch, Sofie was willing to trade it out of vanity. The fool might could use it later for bread or clothing. But then, this Jew had only just arrived. She didn't know what lay ahead. It would serve the fat bitch right if she took the bribe now. In another week, she'll wish she hadn't been so concerned about her dainty arm …

The Pole slid the watch out of Sofie's hand and deftly hid it in the bosom of her shirt. No more words were exchanged as she bent over Sofie's arm.

*"She layeth her hands
to the distaff, And her hands hold
the spindle."*

CHAPTER 10

EMILY METCALF LOOKED OUT of her second-story kitchen window and saw the mailman approaching. She scooped up the baby from his playpen and hurried down the two flights of stairs to the entrance of their apartment building.

"Anything today, Mr. Wilson?" she eagerly asked.

"Now, calm yourself, Miz Metcalf," soothed the old man, "You're gonna upset that li'l fella of yours with all this fuss."

Mr. Wilson pulled an air mail envelope out of his pouch and teased Emily, "Might this be the letter you're so anxious for?"

Emily squealed and grabbed the letter. Clutching both the letter and the baby to her breast, she turned to run back upstairs. She'd climbed about ten steps when she stopped and ran back to Mr. Wilson. She stood on tiptoe to kiss his leathery cheek. He chuckled as he watched her take the stairs two at a time.

She was dying to read the letter first thing, but Peter decided just then that he was hungry. His loud wails made her sigh with impatience as she heated his bottle. After he was fed, she put him down for his nap and tore open the letter. It was the first one she'd received from Russell since he'd shipped out. The past few years had been difficult, what with things in Europe heating up and then the Japs bombing Pearl Harbor. Russell had enlisted in the army right after the attack, as she had known he would. She ruefully smiled at the memory of his nonchalant attitude toward the war during their honeymoon. How carefree they were then!

Before she knew it, he was heading off to army boot camp in Biloxi and she discovered she was expecting their first child. Russell had seen his son only once, on a short leave after he completed basic training. It fell to Emily to run the household and care for their child as best she could by herself. She was coping well enough, but felt awfully alienated from her husband.

Which was why she lived for Russell's letters and his descriptions of what army life was like. She tried to share in his experiences through these infrequent letters, picturing in her mind the scenarios he detailed for her. But her efforts fell short of the kind of intimacy she longed for. This was a part of Russell's life that she really couldn't share, and she resented the barrier the war had placed between them.

"Somewhere in Europe"

December 16, 1943

Dearest Em,

I'd love to be able to tell you where I am, but the good ole censor wouldn't stand for it. So let's just say I'm someplace "bellissima" where I'll take you someday for a second honeymoon. It's kind of ironic that I joined up to fight the Japs and got assigned to the ETO. But believe me, from what I've seen, we were badly needed here. You can't imagine how war ravages, Em.

People, places, lives. Everything is in a shambles. It sure makes our little walk-up look like heaven! Speaking of heaven, how's that boy of mine? Getting to be quite a bruiser, I'll bet. Send me some more snapshots of him, will you, hon? I paste them up wherever I can: my mess kit, inside my helmet, you name it. It helps keep me going on those down days. The scuttlebutt around here is that we'll be heading east before too long. But that's not confirmed yet, so don't go worrying on me, now. Just stay my brave, strong Em and I'll know everything at home is all right. Chow call in five minutes, baby, so I'd better sign off for now. Don't worry if you don't hear from me all that soon. The mails are really getting jerked around.

I love you, Em
Russ

Emily sighed and re-folded the letter along its creases. The last line was true enough; the letter was dated two months ago! But at least she'd heard from him and he was all right. With every newsreel she watched and every radio report she heard, fear welled up anew at the danger Russell was in. But, she thought angrily, at least he was armed and had a fighting chance, unlike those poor creatures at — what was that place called? — Auschwitz. Emily recalled the article she'd read in the *Boston Herald* yesterday. It spoke of the torture and mass murder of Jews and other "undesirables." The horror of it was still with her.

She looked down at her son playing happily in his playpen and babbling that unintelligible baby language understood by no one but himself. She tried to imagine someone taking him from her, doing God knows what …

Impulsively she picked him up and hugged him hard. He let out a yelp of protest and began to whine, but Emily was oblivious to all but the feeling of love that filled her heart. Her child was the recipient of the love she felt for both him and his father. Like Sofie, a woman she hadn't met in a place she could hardly fathom, Emily too was safeguarding a family for her husband.

Stay safe, Russell darling, she thought. But as long as you're there, kick some Nazi butt while you're at it!

Emily could almost hear Russell chuckle in approval.

The Rijnfeld women had been at Auschwitz almost two months. They had all lost weight but were faring well enough. They were still healthy and not overly tormented by the lice problem. Most importantly, they were strong enough to satisfactorily perform their work assignments.

This week, though, the labor had been not only exhausting, but utterly senseless. For 14 hours a day, the women of Block 18 loaded heavy stones into wheelbarrows and moved them from one end of the quarry to the other. There was no real purpose for this activity; the stones simply remained at the new location until the next day when they were once again loaded and wheeled back to their original location.

Work was performed under the watchful eyes of the S. S. If a prisoner failed to move rapidly enough or faltered in her labors, she was whipped. All six Rijnfeld girls were assigned to this job with their stepmother, which gave Sofie mixed feelings. It was gut-wrenching to see the girls struggle under the heavy wheelbarrow, using precious energy on a pointless task intended solely as a means of working them to death. However, as long as they were all together, Sofie could keep an eye on them. If she noticed Elli slowing down, she was able to catch her eye and signal her to keep pace, before the guard caught sight of her lagging behind. When Jopie would have broken down in tears, already succumbing to the harsh treatment, Sofie could sneak a whisper in her ear and convince her not to give the bastards the satisfaction.

The workday was long, for certain, but it never began until the first of two daily roll calls was adequately completed. The prisoners were grouped in four rows of five, multiplied by five, to equal one hundred. This made counting easier for the S. S. officers mounted on horseback as they made their way among the groups. If the numbers didn't tally up, the process could last for hours. One Sunday, they spent the entire day standing in formation while officers counted and recounted. Some prisoners fainted from standing at attention so long in the indian summer heat. A few of the weaker ones collapsed and died in their places, which forced the S. S. to start the count all over again.

It was around four thirty in the morning that the crowded barracks were awakened to the call "*Aus dem Block hinaus! Zählappell!* Come out of the barracks! Roll call!"

Sofie propped herself up on an elbow in her bunk and first made sure that the girls were awake and all right. She always checked on their welfare before she did anything else. Women were packed into three-tiered wooden bunks with flat planks and no mattresses. Sometimes you got a little straw, if you were lucky. Space was at such a premium that if someone turned over, everyone had to turn over. As the prisoner population of Auschwitz grew, more than 1,000 persons were housed in a single barrack originally designed as a stable to house 52 horses.

Not surprisingly, the overcrowding and lack of sanitation resulted in lice infestation. Sofie saw to it that she and her daughters kept as clean as possible with the little water they were rationed each day. A few of her fellow prisoners scoffed at Sofie's attempts to maintain standards that were nearly impossible under such conditions. They laughed and told Sofie she'd best drink her water allotment and forget her primping, or she'd be the cleanest corpse in their block.

Sofie ignored their sarcasm, but part of her wondered if they weren't right. Perhaps she was misguided not to allow the girls to drink all of their water rations. But the inner voice that guided her in these moments of indecision spoke otherwise.

If you give in to the filth, you give in to the degradation. Try as hard as you can to maintain a semblance of normalcy, to keep your dignity.

After roll call, Sofie and the girls swallowed the lukewarm watery liquid that was supposed to be coffee and ate their crusts of stale bread. It was all they would receive until evening, yet they were expected to put in a long day of backbreaking work on this meager sustenance.

There was barely time to run to the latrine before marching to the quarry. Sofie shared the girls' loathing of the latrine, which was nothing more than a long trench dug in the ground. The indignity of it was easier to bear than the sight of the prisoners eating their bread rations while squatting over the wooden plank with the holes cut out at intervals. This evidence of utter dehumanization frightened Sofie. She intuited that if they were to hang on in this place, they must not succumb to the hopelessness of an animal-like existence. Survival depended on it. But how long could they hold out from being beaten down? Depression was beginning to claim all of them.

The day was damp and bleak as the women of Block 18 marched through the ironwork archway that bore the false promise *Arbeit Macht Frei*. A chill in the air foretold of winter, another problem weighing heavily on Sofie's mind. Already she had learned they would receive no additional clothing. How would they keep warm? The women in her block of longer tenure at Auschwitz educated Sofie and the girls about what to expect, and the information was not encouraging.

As they marched, Sofie thought about these other women who had been in the camp for six months and had seen more than Sofie cared to know. She remembered her first week at Auschwitz. She and the girls recoiled in horror at the unnerving sight of a wagonload of corpses en route to the crematoria.

One of the women made an ironic attempt to comfort them.

"You'll get used to it," she soothed. "The first time you see the wagon, you're horrified. The second time you see it, you think, 'Oh, it's the body wagon.' By the third time, you won't even notice it at all."

Sofie knew the woman meant well, but her words were less than comforting. The day she had no reaction to a wagon full of skeletal corpses on the way to the ovens …

The ovens. Shortly after their arrival, the Rijnfelds discovered the source of that sweet, sickish smell permeating the air. Sofie refused to believe it. Although she had met every challenge in her life head-on, this was one possibility to which she turned a blind eye. She knew she was behaving like a child who believes if you can't see what frightens you, it won't be real. But this was one fear she could not face. And was it by design or coincidence that the Germans employed a method of disposition strictly forbidden by Jewish law?

With each passing day, Sofie thought she had seen the worst. But the events of this evening proved she was wrong.

After final roll call, the women settled in for the night as best they could. At the east end of the barracks came the soft strains of a familiar melody that Sofie could not immediately place. Where had she heard it before? Oh, of course — at *shul*. Someone was singing the *Kol Nidre*.

One by one, everyone climbed out of their bunks and went to stand by the woman chanting the haunting melody. Sofie had forgotten all about the High Holidays. Tomorrow was Yom Kippur, the holiest day of the year for Jews.

Although the Rijnfeld family had never been overly religious, they had observed the fast that was required on Yom Kippur, and had attended services. In the midst of this living nightmare, Sofie marveled that the rites of the Holy Days were performed as if nothing was amiss.

Yes, she realized, this is one thing the Nazis can't take from us. We are what we are, and nothing they do will ever change that.

The realization struck her that they were luckier than the Marranos, the secret Jews of the Spanish Inquisition. Forced to choose between conversion to Christianity or death, they appeared to convert while secretly maintaining their Jewish faith and way of life. In Auschwitz there wasn't the option for such a pretense. But the Nazis failed to realize that even as they punished them for being Jews, they enabled them to remain Jews.

Sofie turned to her daughters. "Girls, we forgot all about the Holy Days. Tomorrow we will fast for Yom Kippur."

Anneke was incredulous. "Fast! We're as good as doing that already!"

"Then it won't be much to give up, will it? Anneke dear, we must remember who we are."

"I know who we are, Soof. We're here because of who we are. But I think God will forgive us if we don't fast this year."

"She's right, Soof," Carla put in, "The Nazis may want us to starve, but God doesn't."

The sisters all chimed in, agreeing with Anneke and Carla. Only Mirjam was silent, torn between her hunger and her loyalty to Soof.

Sofie tried again. "Girls, you're all old enough to make up your own minds about this. But I think this year it's more important than ever to hold to our rituals." She looked at the six pairs of eyes that rested on her, some with blatant resentment. "I intend to fast tomorrow. I hope all of you will, too."

For the first time that she could recall, Jopie was furious with her stepmother.

"Rituals!" she sputtered, "Look at us, Soof! Look at Mirjam! We're malnourished already and we don't need to help the Nazis by killing ourselves."

Sofie's voice was quiet. "As I said, Jopie, the choice is yours."

Jopie turned away in disgust. When had Sofie become so pompous? All of a sudden she was so *frum*?

If Jopie had been aware of the self-doubt plaguing Sofie at that moment, she might not have been so hard on her stepmother. The girls returned to their bunks, clearly angry with her. Sofie's throat constricted with the hurt she felt. It wasn't easy to be the strong one all the time, to make choices that affected all their lives. She did what she thought best; couldn't they see that?

Jan's image appeared in her mind's eye. He, too, was angry at her. How can you deny the girls what little morsel they get? he accused. Is this the kind of care you promised me?

Sofie turned away from the image now blurred with tears. She sought only to keep up a sense of normalcy in the midst of this madness. She had also meant to divert the girls' attention from their situation by focusing on something else.

And yes, it was also a matter of pride. To go hungry at God's command was to purify one's soul. To starve at the Nazis' command was merely to die.

When Sofie climbed into her own space in the bunk next to Carla, it was obvious the girls were still upset with her. Sofie stretched out her hand to touch Carla's lank curls in a gesture of truce, but Carla strained out of Sofie's reach. Her unyielding back presented as much a barrier between them as a brick wall.

Maybe Sofie was wrong about the fast, but she felt if she backed down now and changed her mind, her self-imposed position as pillar of strength would be mitigated. And her stepdaughters seemed to forget one thing: she was as hungry as they were.

Sofie fell into a troubled sleep, as much from the emotional turmoil as from physical exhaustion. Just before dawn, the barracks door flung open and the *kapos* charged in, randomly beating the women awake with their knobby sticks. Sofie only glanced at the girls to inventory their condition, then quickly turned away. For the first time in her adult life, she felt very vulnerable and alone.

She sighed as she stepped into her wooden clogs. It was going to be a particularly difficult day. She hadn't realized how much her own courage was fueled by her stepdaughters' support and their need for a figurehead.

Her thoughts were interrupted by one of the female S. S. guards. She was a Brunhilde of a woman who was reputed to be as cold as ice. She entered the barracks trailed by a *kapo* carrying a large carton.

"We have a special treat for you today, *frauen*," said the guard. "This morning you will each receive a whole slice of bread with marmalade."

Her grin was malevolent as she gestured to the *kapo* to distribute the bread. She knew what day it was. She knew it would be particularly hard for some of the more religious Jews to eat that bread, as hard as it would be for them to forego it. It was a lose-lose situation for the prisoners, and the guard reveled in it.

While the prisoners eagerly crowded around to receive their pieces of bread, Sofie questioned one of them.

"Why are they so solicitous of us, all of a sudden? Is the bread poisoned or something?"

"I don't know and I don't care," the woman replied, "If it's offered, I'm going to eat it."

Sofie saw her stepdaughters among the throng clamoring for the extra rations. Only Elli caught her eye, anger written plainly on her face. Anneke stepped back from the crush with bread in hand, smacking her lips in anticipation of the treat. She noticed Sofie standing to one side, and set her mouth in defiance.

The message was clear. The girls had made their choice, and resented their stepmother's.

Sofie turned away. Their ostracism pained her more than her empty belly.

A raspy voice came from behind. An emaciated woman of about 45 with large circles under eyes set in a sunken face stood in a corner. She rocked back and forth, crooning to herself and holding a clenched fist to her breast. At frequent intervals she thumped her fist against her breast, all the while *davening* the *Al Chet*, the recitation of one's sins. She intoned the traditional Yom Kippur prayer unmindful of the delicious bread and marmalade being doled out. As Sofie watched her, her own stomach growled with a vengeance, needlessly reminding her of her constant hunger.

Sofie felt a hand touch her shoulder. She turned to find Mirjam smiling at her, her outstretched hand proffering a thick slice of black bread spread with orange marmalade. She could see bits of orange rind in it.

A peace offering? A show of spite? Sofie's ears caught part of the litany of sins the praying woman enumerated.

" ... and for the sin of spurning our parents and teachers, for the sin of spreading gossip, for the sin of being stiff-necked ... "

"Soof?" Mirjam proffered the bread again.

Without a word, Sofie took the bread and devoured it.

"She maketh for herself coverlets; Her clothing is fine linen and purple"

CHAPTER 11

KOMMANDANTUR RUDOLF HÖSS GLANCED out the window on this cold but sunny morning while he waited for his guests. About once a month he breakfasted in his quarters with several of his higher-ranking officers, finding that it helped keep up morale. Many of the officers had elected not to bring their families along to the *konzentrationslager*, fearing the climate would be too inhospitable. As a result, some felt lonely and isolated so far away from home. But an elaborate repast in the *kommandantur's* plush quarters was always something to write home about. Höss also used these informal gatherings as an opportunity to glean information on the daily running of the camp — things he might not read about in official reports.

He leaned back contentedly in his chair as a Jewess in a black maid's uniform refilled his coffee cup. There was no denying that he, too, enjoyed the fine meals prepared for these breakfast meetings. An aficionado of gourmet cuisine, Höss enjoyed not only the food itself but a certain smugness at being able to procure such wartime delicacies as gravlax, steak and kidney pie, and fresh-squeezed orange juice. The members of his staff rarely ate this well even during peacetime, so it was no surprise than an invitation to breakfast with *Herr Kommandantur* was a much coveted honor.

Höss stirred his coffee and took a cigarette from the silver case in his jacket pocket. The captain seated to his right was quick to light it for him.

He smiled at his guests. "Nothing like a good hot breakfast to start a cold day, eh, gentlemen?" Smiles and polite nods of concurrence went around the mahogany table.

Höss curiously eyed a young captain seated at the far end. "What ails you, Fritz? Was something not to your liking?"

"*Nein, Herr Kommandantur.* The meal was excellent. It's just — " The sentence hung unfinished in the clouds of cigarette smoke.

"Speak up, my boy. What's on your mind?" Höss' tone became paternal.

Fritz hesitated, then took the plunge. "I've put in for a transfer, *Herr Kommandantur.*"

The surprise of the other officers showed on their faces and murmured reactions held forth.

Höss raised his forefinger to the maid for more coffee all around. She poured from a silver pot into the Dresden china cups. Höss crushed out his cigarette in a crystal ashtray and folded his hands on the table, leaning forward with concern.

"But why, Fritz?" he asked, "You've done very well in your duties here. I was under the impression that you had waited a long time to be assigned to Auschwitz. Have you not been happy in this post?"

"It's not that, sir," Fritz replied, "I am very honored to have been recommended for this assignment. But to be honest, *Herr Kommandantur*, I am a soldier. I want to be fighting at the front, not in the rear supervising men who supervise Jews."

"An understandable desire. But yours is an important job, Fritz. Good leaders such as you are vital to the Reich, else how can we succeed in eliminating the Jewish burden on society?"

"Exactly the point, sir," Fritz went on earnestly, "I want more of an active role in the elimination of the *Juden*. I can't do that sitting in an office."

Höss smiled his understanding. "Ah, now I see. You want to take out some of the swine yourself, eh?"

"I admit it's true, sir. When my knife runs with Jewish blood, I'll be content."

A loud rattle of china came from the sideboard where the maid was stacking dishes. Thankfully, nothing had broken but she knew she had called attention to herself, and feared Höss' wrath. It was just that the young officer had spoken with such serene venom that her hands had involuntarily started to shake.

Fritz smiled to himself in satisfaction, knowing his words had affected the girl. He had spoken them especially for her benefit, so she wouldn't think herself exempt from her ultimate destiny simply because she was lucky enough to be working as *Herr Kommandant's* maid. The other officers paid no attention to the fact that their meal was served by a Jewish whore, nor did they consider that she could hear every word of their references to elimination of the Jews. Still, it angered Fritz to see a Jew have it so easy.

Too bad she hadn't dropped a dish or cup; Fritz might have been granted permission to administer the beating himself.

Höss pushed his chair back from the table and resumed the conversation. "If that's all you find lacking in your service to the *Führer*, we can easily remedy that."

Höss turned to the dapper officer seated on his left. "Josef, think you could put Fritz to good use in your department?"

The officer nodded his assent. "Most certainly, *Herr Kommandantur.* We can always use willing helpers. In fact, I have a selection scheduled for this morning. Perhaps the captain would like to come along? See how it's done?"

Fritz was almost boyish in his excitement. He stood up to face the officer, clicked his heels together and gave a little bow. "Thank you, *Herr* Mengele!" He turned toward Höss and repeated the gesture. "And thank you, *Herr Kommandantur*, for taking such a personal interest in my assignment."

"Contented soldiers are efficient soldiers, Fritz. I'm sure the *Führer* would not want such enthusiasm to be wasted."

Dr. Josef Mengele's *selektions* were infamous at Auschwitz. Conducted periodically to weed out those prisoners too weak or too ill to work, the process made room for newer arrivals who would be more productive. The Nazis had calculated that, on the small rations allotted, prisoners at hard labor would survive three to six months. This method not only provided laborers for the Reich, but complied with the "Final Solution to the Jewish Question."

Sofie had heard about the *selektions*, but thus far her luck had held out. There had not been a selection in the women's camp since her arrival at Auschwitz. Luck often had a great deal to do with the outcome of these selections. To satisfy *Herr Doktor* and be spared from the gas chamber, you had to be flawless. This meant much more than merely cheating starvation. Even a pimple or a boil was enough to render you "selected."

Block 18 was in a flurry of activity. Sofie wondered why they had not been ordered to line up for the march to the quarry, as usual.

One of the women enlightened her. "There's going to be a *selektion*. Hurry and fix yourself up! You want to look healthy and strong, don't you?"

"What the — "

Sofie left her question unfinished and unanswered as she scurried back and forth in a dither, unsure of what to do, but thinking that she should do something. Presently it dawned on her: there was nothing to fear. She and the girls were still strong enough to work and were free of illness, thank God. There was no reason why any of her family should be selected.

Sofie saw the woman she had just spoken with rubbing something vigorously into her skin. She noticed Sofie's bemused expression.

"Margarine," she explained, "I save a little from my rations and use it as a balm. It helps the cracking."

"Don't you think you should eat it instead?" Sofie asked, taking in the woman's gaunt frame.

The woman shrugged. "The better I look, the better my chances."

Sofie shook her head in disbelief and the woman continued, "You think I'm the only *meshuggeh*? Look over there."

Sofie turned to a group of French women in a corner of the barracks busily scooping up small amounts of dry dirt from the floor into their cupped hands. They spit into their palms and mixed the dirt into a paste which they carefully applied to their eyebrows. Lacking mirrors, they performed the task for one another.

Leave it to the French to primp for a *selektion*, Sofie thought. Still, perhaps they had the right idea …

Sofie beckoned to her daughters and quickly did as she saw the French women do. There was little time for explanations, and luckily the girls did not press her. One by one, she made up the six girls. No sooner had she finished applying the paste to Anneke when the *kapo* shouted for them to line up outside. There had been no time for Sofie to darken her own eyebrows; she would just have to make it without it.

Outside, a frigid wind blew through Sofie's matted hair. She saw Lena blink hard against the specks of dirt that crumbled as it dried on her eyebrows and fell into her eyes. A small table and two chairs stood in the clearing to one side of the barracks. An S. S. sergeant sat at the table, making notes on a clipboard. Next to him stood Dr. Mengele, tall and pristine in his spotless uniform, well-guarded against the cold by a heavy cloth coat. A eager-looking younger officer stood beside him. He appeared to be anticipating the selection with great pleasure.

Mengele nodded to the *kapo*, who in turn shouted at the women to strip off their clothes. Those who did not comply with sufficient haste received blows from the *kapo's* stick. The Rijnfeld girls glanced questioningly at Sofie, who gave them the slightest nod. Hesitantly, they all began to remove their scanty clothing.

All except Lena.

Ever since Klaus had raped her at Westerbork, Lena had become reluctant for anyone to see her unclothed, even her stepmother and sisters. When they had first arrived at Auschwitz, Lena had gone into hysterics when forced to strip for delousing. She calmed down only when a guard threatened to shoot her.

On the rare occasion when she washed, she did so in the darkest corner of the barracks, her back to the room. Sofie feared that forcing Lena to strip now might break her completely. But she was more afraid of what would happen if she refused.

Standing next to Lena, Elli helped her step out of her shift. At her sister's touch, Lena recoiled and clutched the dress tightly to her, violently shaking her head no. The *kapo* saw the commotion and came over with stick raised, ready to shut them up with a few blows, if necessary. At his approach, Lena regained her composure as abruptly as she had lost it. She threw aside Elli's helping hand and removed her dress, her eyes fixed on the ground.

Sofie was immensely relieved. No matter how great the indignation, her motto was always to remain unobtrusive. Attracting undue attention from the Nazis spelled disaster.

The bitter wind struck Sofie like a knife, penetrating the naked body that was no longer plump. Her breasts hung slack against ribs clearly outlined. Her hip bones stuck out sharply against her skin. But she was unmindful of the metamorphosis her body had undergone, oblivious to the fact that she stood naked for the perusal of men who would judge her worthy or not to remain alive. She knew only the cold that pierced her very bones. She tried hard not to shiver, aware that she had no spare energy to waste on a futile attempt to keep warm. How much longer would they have to stand there, freezing?

As if in answer, the *kapo* shouted at the women to file past the table. Sofie stole a glance back at her daughters and received a cuff on the head for her effort. Though she deplored having to parade naked in front of these Nazis like a horse up for auction, she was glad at least to be moving. Even this minor exertion was better than standing at attention in the icy wind. She kept her eyes focused forward, but felt Mengele's scrutiny as she passed. Her hollow cheeks reddened with more than the bite of the wind.

It seemed ages before she was safely past the table. But the ordeal was not yet over. At a signal from Mengele, the *kapo* shouted, "Faster, faster, faster!"

The weak and exhausted women no longer had the dexterity to instantly change their gait, and a pile-up ensued. Had it not been so horrible, it would almost have been comical, like a burlesque bit.

Sofie found herself pressed up against Carla's back and took advantage of the proximity to poke a finger into her side.

"Stand up," she hissed in Carla's ear, "Step high."

Still annoyed with her stepmother over the fasting issue, Carla fumed silently. Soof was turning into a self-righteous slave driver while she was nothing more than a slave herself! Carla intended to give her a piece of her mind when they returned to the barracks. Meanwhile, she used her impotent anger to fuel her cold and tired body. She straightened her spine and brought her knees high as she jogged past Mengele.

None of the Rijnfelds noticed when Mengele pointed at one or another of the women as they passed by. After they were told to halt and put their clothes back on, they noticed some women lined up apart from the group who resumed formation. The selectees were mostly the older women of Block 18, all emaciated and feeble. They were silent as the S.S. guard led them away, their hollow eyes staring blankly.

"Where are they taking them?" Mirjam whispered, "Why aren't they going with us?"

Sofie wasn't sure. Just as she started to reply, the woman on her other side answered Mirjam's question.

"They're going to be gassed," she said dully.

Sofie grabbed Mirjam's hand and held it fast, annoyed at the woman's tactlessness. Mirjam knew better than to react audibly to this revelation while still in formation, but she clenched Sofie's hand like a vise.

Those who had made it through selection were kept standing until the victims were almost out of sight. Sofie saw the woman who had been chanting *Kol Nidre* at the rear of the line. She felt certain the woman was now reciting *Kaddish*.

Mengele and the young captain walked down the line. Mengele seemed to be instructing the younger officer in something. He stopped midway and lifted his cane toward the six sisters. He murmured something to the officer and the two laughed together. Mengele's face sobered as he looked at directly at Lena. He brought his hand to her face.

Lena recoiled.

Mengele held his palm up in a non-threatening gesture. He was gentle as he ran his thumb across her brow. He viewed the dirt that came away on his thumb and showed it to the captain.

"Your face is dirty, *fraulein*," he remarked casually to Lena. She stood still, unsure what was expected of her.

The captain offered his own handkerchief to the doctor, but Mengele declined. He made two diagonal strokes on Lena's forehead with his thumb, the residual dirt forming an X.

"The scarlet letter," he quipped.

The captain laughed appropriately and proffered the handkerchief once again. Mengele accepted it this time and wiped the dirt off his hand as they walked away. He handed it back to the captain, who tossed it over his shoulder.

"Let the Jew girl have it," he called to the S. S. guard, "She may want to 'freshen up.'"

Lena waited until they were out of sight before she dared move. But she didn't retrieve the handkerchief. With a trembling hand, she wiped the black smudge from her face. High above her in the sky, a large bird — a hawk, maybe — soared in a wide arc. It was the only bird she'd seen the entire time they'd been in the camp. Lena stared at it with envy. How marvelous to be able to go wherever you want.

Envy quickly turned to resentment. Why can an ugly black bird have freedom and she could not? What awful thing had she done to deserve this?

In an unreasonable act of rebellious rage, Lena bent down and grabbed a fistful of dirt. As hard as she could, she flung it skyward at the bird. The wild swing of her arm threw her off balance and she fell to the ground. Sofie bent to gather her in her arms and take her back to the barracks before her actions brought repercussions. In between sobs, Lena gulped, "Why the bird and not me?"

Sofie hadn't seen the bird and didn't understand the reference. All she knew was that a small chink had appeared in the armor in which she had tried to encase her daughters. She tried not to think about how long would it be before the Nazis discovered and took advantage of it.

"Her husband is known in the gates,
When he sitteth among
the elders of the land."

CHAPTER 12

WINTER MELTED INTO SPRING, but at Auschwitz the annual promise of life's renewal was lost on those who struggled to hang on to their very existence. The only flowers peeping green shoots through the soil were in front of the German officers' quarters, far removed from the realities of the camp. In Sofie's realm of consciousness, no trees sprouted new leaves. No cacophony of hungry birdlings in their nests rang in her ears. There was only bleakness.

With the change of seasons, the Rijnfeld women grew weaker. They had thus far escaped the typhus raging through the women's camp, a small miracle in their condition. Nonetheless, their malnourished bodies told the tale of their situation. Jopie was covered with scabs from constant scratching where the lice tormented her. Anneke had developed a cough that wouldn't disappear. Lena frequently drifted in and out of a silent world of her own, one that became more and more difficult for her sisters to penetrate. Mirjam, Elli, and Carla were very weak, but surviving.

Sofie, too, was weak from hunger but she forbade herself to give in to it. She was not so naïve as to pretend that her self-imposed responsibility to the girls wasn't critical to her own survival. The promise she had made to Jan carried her through the times when she thought she could stand no more. Every now and then, a prisoner who no longer had the will to go on would throw herself against the electrified fence that surrounded the camp. The first time she witnessed this, Sofie was horrified. The past month or two, it became an option she considered more than once.

It was times like that when Sofie's thoughts of her husband turned bitter. She imagined Jan sitting in their comfortable home, and resentment festered. How could he just let his wife go off like that, to God knows where? If he really loved her, he would never have agreed to let her go, to put her in this position. The girls were his children, after all.

Come to think of it, he had agreed without much argument at all. What kind of lily livered man was he? He barely protested when she announced her intention to go with the girls. Fine for him; he gets to stay safe and warm at home while Sofie took on the obligation of his daughters' welfare.

A thought struck her. Was this the real reason Jan had married her — to fill a mother's shoes? Maybe her own mother had been right to caution her against marrying a man with six children ...

Sofie's heart grew hot with these musings. When the war ended and she got out of here, she'd have a thing or two to discuss with Jan Rijnfeld. Whether she could love him again after this experience, she wasn't sure.

Yes, she'd deal with Jan much later. Right now, she had other worries on her mind ... like staying alive.

Sofie's chief worry at present was Lena. She was slipping farther and farther away from reality, a situation Sofie wasn't sure how to contend with. To keep the other girls strong of mind, she talked to all of them as often as possible about art, music, anything but the food and clothing they didn't have. But Lena's fragile mental state was unresponsive to this simple strategy.

Summer came and brought with it a heat that made the backbreaking work in the quarry more intolerable. They were given small amounts of water at midday, and Sofie often gave her ration to whichever of the girls needed it most. There were days, though, when she kept the water for herself, reasoning that a dead stepmother was no good to them.

On one of those days, an S. S. guard approached Sofie as she drank

122

her water ration. She immediately snapped to attention and waited for the punishment she was sure was coming for some imagined infraction.

To her surprise, the guard just stood casually before her. He didn't look angry. What now?

The guard wiped his sleeve across his sweaty forehead. "Hot today, isn't it, *Frau*?"

Sofie was confused by this uncharacteristic small talk. "Yes, sir," she hesitated, remaining at attention.

The guard smiled at her. "You know, you're not going to survive this," he said amiably. "You know that, don't you? I will make sure of it myself. But if by chance you do survive, nobody will believe you. Nobody will believe what we did to you people."

With that, he ambled off. Sofie kept stock still even after he was gone. The enormity of what he said frightened her, as she was sure had been his intention.

But what if he wasn't merely trying to intimidate? What if he was right?

Oh God, why had she been so hasty in deciding to accompany the girls? She hadn't given much thought to the possible consequences, and now it was too late. Her oh-so-noble gesture was moot if they all ended up dead …

At the end of the day, the women were marched back from the quarry a little earlier than usual. There were still a few hours of daylight left, but Sofie didn't question this departure from routine. She was too grateful to be relieved of the day's labor. As they passed through the iron archway, Sofie heard the strains of a lively march played by the camp orchestra. Returning workers were expected to step smartly to the beat of the music. Usually, Sofie took pains to ensure that her girls did so. This afternoon, though, it was all she could do not to collapse, herself. Physical exhaustion and the emotional toll taken by the guard's chilling prophecy had drained her completely. She concentrated on putting one foot in front of the other, and by some miracle made it back to barracks.

As they neared Block 18, Sofie became lightheaded at the hope of resting on her bunk for a few minutes before evening roll call. Even the unyielding wooden planks that crawled with lice could not detract from her anticipation. But no sooner had they halted in front of their barracks when a *kapo* shouted for them to line up and undress for *selektion*.

Frantic whispers went through the ranks as the women realized there would be no chance to "fix up." As Sofie mechanically removed her dress, she saw a French girl surreptitiously cut her fingertip on a sharp stone. She rubbed a drop of blood into each cheek. A barbarous rouge.

Sofie made to help Lena off with her dress, primed for the usual struggle. Poor Lena relived the trauma she had experienced at the hands of Klaus every time she was forced to undress. But surprisingly, this time Lena made no move to resist. She stood placid and uncaring while Sofie pulled the shift down to her ankles and helped her step out of it.

The women began their sordid parade in front of the S. S., breaking into a trot at the *kapo's* command. Sofie was behind Lena, nudging her, prodding her into a trot. But Lena just halted and stared blankly at Sofie.

The *kapo* gave Lena's face a vicious slap for her idleness. She only stared. The S. S. officers in charge bent their heads together in conference. They signaled the *kapo* to remove Lena from the line-up. She was led away, still naked, while the selection resumed.

Sofie broke free and ran to the table where the officers sat.

"No!" she protested, oblivious to her own nudity and the danger her outburst presented. "You can't take her! She's fine; she can still work!"

"Do you want to go with her, Mother?" the S. S. officer asked.

Immediately, Sofie saw the folly in her pleading. If she went with Lena, she would be deserting the rest of the family, as well as signing her own death warrant. For their own protection, she must stay and live.

"No, please, *Herr Kapitan*," Sofie stammered, "I — I only meant that she still could work."

The officer gave Sofie an appraising look. He should send her to the ovens for her outburst, but he hated to waste viable manpower. This one had a month or two of work left in her.

"Get back in line," he growled, returning to his paperwork.

Sofie quickly returned to formation, where Lena's sisters were weeping softly. After the selection of two more women, Sofie and the others hurriedly dressed.

No one said a word about what had just taken place.

Lena was put in the back of a truck with a dozen or so other women who had also been selected. All were so weak or sick that they didn't even look up at the naked girl who seemed not to comprehend what was happening.

As the truck pulled away, Lena lifted her face to the warm sun and felt the sweet air rushing around her. It was such a lovely day for a ride. Funny, she couldn't remember that Pappie had traded their sedan for a convertible. But Lena didn't care; it had been so long since she'd gone for a drive.

The truck pulled up in front of a large brick building with no windows. The selectees were ordered off and they filed listlessly inside, where they were told to undress for a shower.

Hang your clothing on the pegs on the wall, they were told. It will be deloused and returned to you afterward.

A prisoner assigned to this detail gathered up the discarded clothing, barely glancing at the naked scarecrows. They were herded into a square room with shower nozzles mounted into the ceiling.

Before he shut the airtight door, an S. S. officer urged them, "Breathe deeply. The steam will be good for you."

Lena frowned that her pleasant outing was cut short just to take a shower. Still, it would be nice to wash her hair. Fingering it, she wondered how it had gotten in such bad shape. She would have to get a permanent as soon as she got home.

She found herself crushed against the other women crowded into the small room. The heavy door closed them in and was locked into place with rotating handles. She heard a "ping," and then a hiss of steam. Ah, how good a nice hot shower will feel!

She coughed. It was getting hard to breathe. Why was the steam so thick? Some of the women began screaming and clutching their throats, eyes bulging. Lena's lungs felt like they were being stuffed with cotton. She gagged and choked, straining to gulp air.

In their panic, the women began trampling one another, trying to climb above the choking gas and find some breathable air. Lena lost her footing when an hysterical woman grabbed wildly at whomever was near. She fell to her knees and the panicking victim stepped on her back in her efforts to escape the poison gas. Lena's frail body crumpled under the added weight and she rolled over, still gagging.

Mammie! Please help me, Mammie!

She felt a great pressure on her chest as others heedlessly stepped on her, driven by their own instincts to escape the choking fumes. Their cries and screams reached Lena's ears more faintly now, as if coming from far away. The pressure on her chest grew heavier. Her field of vision narrowed smaller and smaller until only a pinpoint of light danced before her eyes.

A last convulsive jerk, and she was still.

"She maketh linen garments and selleth them; And delivereth girdles unto the merchant."

CHAPTER 13

THROUGHOUT THE SUMMER OF 1944, the Nazis reached their peak of killing in the death camps, thousands every day. The S. S. personnel who carried out this methodically orchestrated genocide saw nothing unusual in the task. The annihilation was performed totally devoid of emotion. As Himmler often said, they did not hate the Jews, so what was there to be emotional about?

The way he saw it, the obliteration of the Jews was merely a logical sequence of events. If you merely hate people, you get furious. You might work off the hatred if you manage to kill a few. But if you can translate murder into rules, regulations, bureaucracy, and technology, it can continue on and on, with no moral recriminations. After all, a Jew is a Jew, like a herring is a herring.

But Himmler had not anticipated that, toward the end of 1944, Germany would be losing the war. As the Allies advanced, the Nazis were forced to speed up the killing in the camps while cutting expenses in the process. They met this challenge by decreasing the use of costly Zyklon B, the prussic acid used in the gas chambers. They began burning Jews alive, many of them just children.

The very real possibility of losing the war forced the Nazis to deal with another problem. The mass graves containing the slaughtered victims in concentration camps all over eastern Europe contained tangible evidence of Hitler's "Final Solution." It certainly wouldn't do to have them discovered. Better to open the graves and burn the corpses.

The crematoria fires were kept going night and day as the corpses were exhumed and reduced to ashes along with the fresh corpses dumped on top. Though the crematoria worked constantly, they still could not keep pace with the demand. Ultimately, they had to resort to open-air pyres, burning over 2,000 bodies a day.

Sofie did her best to turn a blind eye to what was happening, but the stench of burning flesh did not allow the luxury of closing one's eyes. Among the prisoners still alive, rumor had it that the frenzied disposal of bodies meant liberation was at hand. Sofie badly needed to hold on to that crumb of hope, but it couldn't dispel her grief in remembering that Lena had been reduced to ashes by the same flames that might be illuminating her salvation. Anneke, Jopie, and Elli were gone too, one by one, having been selected for gassing. Their wasted bodies lay somewhere in the endless mounds of corpses burning throughout the camp.

Fortunately, Sofie never knew that Elli had not been quite dead when she was removed with the other victims from the gas chamber and trucked to the crematorium. A young male prisoner, whose gruesome task was to shovel the corpses into the ovens, heard Elli's soft moans coming from the heap of dead bodies he was preparing to burn. He examined the corpses to try to locate the sound. The low moans led him to Elli lying like a rag doll in the middle, bodies piled on top of her. Her eyes were only half open, but they were aware.

He immediately reported his discovery to the *kapo*, who gave a scornful laugh and ordered him to keep on loading the ovens.

"But this one's still alive!"

The *kapo* cuffed him on the head. "You make sure that body is the next one you put in the oven, or I'll personally see to it that you'll go next."

The prisoner returned to his post. Elli was moaning more softly now, like a mewling kitten. The thought of the choice he had to make sickened him. But there really was no choice. He pulled Elli from the mound of corpses and placed her on a long wooden paddle. He turned his head away from her face. If he saw her eyes, he knew he'd never be able to go through with it. He opened the chamber door of the oven and reeled from the blast of heat. Desperate to drown out the sound of Elli's moaning, he started to sing the first song lyrics that popped into his head. He picked up the paddle — it weighed next to nothing with Elli's starved body — and positioned it on the edge of the oven floor. In one swift movement, he shoved it all the way in and shut the door.

Falling to his knees, he vomited.

Despite Sofie's best efforts to see her daughters through this nightmare, only Carla and Mirjam remained with her, and they were extremely weak. Carla had contracted typhus and was very ill. Sofie tried to nurse them, but her resources were practically nonexistent. She spared whatever liquid rations of her own that she could without putting herself on the brink of collapse. When Carla became too weak to stand for roll-call, she was removed to the *krankhaus*, the camp infirmary. It was widely known that "infirmary" was a misnomer, for no one transferred there ever recovered. It was not widely known that most of the *krankhaus* patients were given injections of air into their veins, or lethal doses of Pentothal.

Once Carla was taken away, Mirjam grew even weaker. Sofie hadn't told her the whole truth about her sisters' deaths, but Mirjam sensed what had happened. With all of them gone, she lost most of her own will to live. Sofie had believed that if anyone could make it, it was her plucky Mirjam. But nothing she did or said seemed to help the girl rally.

Sofie observed the young woman wasting away on a filthy wooden bunk and silently raged that her youth had been spent like this. When they first entered the camps, Mirjam had been fifteen. She never had a chance to know the excitement of a first date, the wonder of a first kiss. At a time in her life when she should have been fussing over hair styles and party dresses, Mirjam was struggling to move heavy rocks from one place to another. The injustice of it all frustrated Sofie more than she could stand.

Mirjam spoke weakly. "Soof?"

Sofie took up her hand. "Yes, darling. I'm here"

"Why did God let this happen? Why doesn't He put an end to it?"

Why, indeed, Sofie thought. She'd asked herself the same question countless times, searching for some explanation that might rationalize this madness. She tried to comfort Mirjam with the only answer she could think of to such an unanswerable question, but it sounded ludicrous to her own ears even as she spoke the words.

"Don't blame God, darling. It's not His fault. He gave human beings free will, but He can't control what they do with it. He can only offer His strength to those who suffer by others' abuse of it."

Sofie turned her head in disgust at her own words. What pompous crap! She sounded like some sort of prison chaplain doling out platitudes.

Tears spilled from her eyes as she lay down next to Mirjam, trying to warm her with her own meager body heat. She was enervated beyond endurance — a chronic condition — but afraid to sleep, with Mirjam so sick. In spite of herself, exhaustion took over and sleep came. When she awoke, it was still dark, but she sensed it was almost time for morning roll-call.

As had been her ritual since their arrival at Auschwitz, Sofie first checked on her stepdaughter. When she touched Mirjam's cheek, it felt cold and strange. She put two fingers to her neck over the carotid artery, and waited.

Nothing.

Sofie slumped over Mirjam's still body.

Gone. All six girls.

She took Mirjam's hand in her own and brought it to her chest, rocking back and forth as she cradled the lifeless limb. It was then that Sofie noticed something clutched in Mirjam's hand. She pried open the already stiffening fingers and pulled out a wrinkled piece of paper. There was writing on it, scratchy and faded.

> *I believe in the sun even when it is not shining,*
> *I believe in love even when not feeling it,*
> *I believe in God even when God is silent.*

Sofie wondered where this had come from. She didn't bother to ask around, though. Someone had thought to bring comfort to a dying girl. For Sofie, that was enough.

Sofie never knew how she made it through roll call that morning. She forced herself to stand in formation and not utter a sound while the body wagon drove away with Mirjam on top of the heap of corpses.

Roll call took less time now, as more and more prisoners died or were killed. Sofie had to stand in the crisp November air for only one hour this morning before the tally was confirmed. As she marched to work in the quarry, she took note that, of the original group of women in Block 18 assigned to this job, she was the only one left. Her preoccupation with her daughters had eclipsed all else, but now that they were gone it was like being back after a long absence.

She miserably observed her newer co-workers. They were all younger and healthier, having arrived more recently. Sofie regretted that she stood out as an example of what these women could look forward to in a few months. On the other hand, her natural optimism pointed to her as living testimony to the will to survive. She chose to focus on the latter.

The morning was still young when a freezing rain began to fall. The women were expected to continue working at the same pace, but most found it difficult to hold onto the rocks with hands that were stiff from the cold.

Her wheelbarrow full, Sofie took up the handles to push the heavy cart to the quarry's other side where she would unload her quota. Before she could muster the force to move the rock-laden wheelbarrow, an S. S. guard shouted at her.

"Halt!"

Sofie quickly laid the handles on the ground and stood at attention.

The guard sauntered over to her and insolently inspected her as she stood straight as a ramrod, eyes forward.

He pointed to the stones in the wheelbarrow. "Where do you think you were going with these?"

Perplexed, Sofie answered, "To unload them on the other side, sir."

The guard picked up a rock and played it back and forth between his hands, judging its weight.

"You worthless cow of a Jew! You re supposed to move rocks, not pebbles!"

He overturned Sofie's wheelbarrow, the stones cascading into a pile at Sofie's feet.

"Begin again, and this time do it right." He tossed the rock he was holding on top of the pile. The other guards laughed.

Sofie had trouble containing her anger. She pursed her lips and forced herself not to react. She permitted herself a glance at her tormentor, and found herself looking into the cold eyes of Klaus.

That night, Sofie lay in her bunk, unable to sleep. Klaus, the sadistic guard who had raped Lena and unhinged her mind, was here at Auschwitz. Was it coincidence that he should be transferred here, or did he request it to reclaim Lena as his personal plaything? She was glad that Lena was beyond Klaus' reach in a place where he couldn't hurt her anymore.

But Sofie was still here, and she remembered the blow Klaus gave her at Westerbork when she had tried to protect Lena. She was sure Klaus remembered it too. Now he would want more. This morning had been a preview of what was to come, she was certain. Klaus had savored springing this surprise reunion on her, and would no doubt single her out for future "infractions."

When Klaus had laid her low with one fist at Westerbork, she had been relatively strong and healthy. In her present condition, she wouldn't last long if he acted on his vendetta. The irony was not lost on Sofie. Had she come through all this only to die at the hands of one vengeful Nazi soldier?

She wanted very much to live, but she knew it was in God's hands now. All the optimism in the universe wouldn't protect her from Klaus. She would tread softly and hope that nothing would go awry, but Klaus would be sure to find fault with something — anything — in order to punish her.

Please, God, she prayed, if it does happen, don't let me suffer long. Let it be over quickly. She found new satisfaction in her prayer. He'd find nothing more frustrating than for me to die before he's had his fun. Then he'd have to find something else to occupy his time.

Sofie felt a little calmer now. She could go to sleep. If she died quickly from Klaus' special attentions, she would deny him the satisfaction of making her suffer. If she survived, she thwarted his revenge.

Either way, Klaus didn't beat her. Klaus didn't win.

All the next day at the quarry, Sofie remained braced for Klaus to strike at any given moment. She cast furtive glances at him now and then, surprised that he didn't harass her. In fact, he hardly looked her way. He joked with the other guards when he joined them for a quick smoke. He rubbed his cold hands together over the makeshift fire another guard built. He laughed when an exhausted woman prisoner stumbled under the weight of her wheelbarrow.

But he paid no attention to Sofie.

The winter sun sank lower, and the steam whistle signaled the end of the workday. Sofie permitted herself to relax a little as she assembled with the others for the march back to camp. Klaus hadn't bothered with her all day.

The exhausted group of women marched mechanically through the main gate. Thank God they didn't have to stop for inspection like the prisoners returning from work in the fields and orchards. Every night, those poor souls were detained at the gate and bodily searched. Anyone caught smuggling in a forbidden potato or apple on her person was made an example to the others. The usual consequence was a severe beating, but a few were hanged to drive home the message more clearly.

Sofie's group was startled out of its zombie-like state when they were commanded to halt just inside the main gate.

Someone has been smuggling bread into the camp, they were informed. All prisoners returning from work outside the fence were subject to search, regardless of the nature of their job.

Nobody displayed any reaction to this development, but Sofie felt the despair of the others — as well as her own — at this needless delay. Where would any of them find bread in a rock quarry?

The guard passed among the prisoners in search of the contraband. Sofie raised her arms high above her head, ready to be inspected. She paid little heed to the proceedings, thinking only of the tepid gruel soon to be doled out.

The guard's triumphant cry made her start, while the strong jab of his rifle butt in her side made her double over. He yanked Sofie out of line and shoved her to the front where the other guards were.

"This is the one. She had it in her pocket." The guard held out a small crust of bread to show the others.

Again the rifle butt plowed into Sofie's middle, causing her to moan in pain. She bent over and clutched her abdomen, her eyes level with a pair of boots, one foot casually crossed over the other. When the pain subsided, she straightened up slowly, breathing hard. Her gaze rose the length of the figure that leaned easily against the iron gate, arms folded across his chest. The steely look on his face explained it all.

"Bring her in," Klaus said, "We'll teach these Jews what happens to thieves in Auschwitz."

Sofie was half dragged, half pushed into the punishment block. Klaus followed behind, pleased with the success of his plan. It was worth the extra cigarette rations he had to pay Dieter for his help in the "discovery" of the smuggler. But war inspired greed, and Klaus understood Dieter's asking price. Considering the pleasure he was about to have paying back that Jew whore, it was a bargain …

Hell, thought Klaus, if it were me, I'd have done it for nothing, just for the fun of watching a Jew beg and plead.

The two guards pulled Sofie to the middle of a bare room where a small wooden table stood. They shoved her over the table, face down. Each man grabbed an arm on either side, holding her down.

Klaus went over to where she stood sprawled across the table. In his hand was thick rubber hose. His eyes gleamed.

"For your crime of smuggling, you will receive twenty lashes with this hose," he declared. "You will count off the strokes yourself, Jew bitch, out loud in German."

Sofie tried to raise her head to look at Klaus, but the guards yanked her arms forward, slamming her face against the table. Her words came muffled. "I don't speak German."

Klaus cocked his ear toward her. "You say something, Jew? I can't hear you."

Sofie's breath came fast and shallow as she struggled to speak louder. "I don't know any German … sir."

Klaus flexed the rubber hose. "Well, then, I'm afraid I won't know when I'm supposed to stop, will I?"

Without preamble, the hose came down on Sofie's back with the force of a whip and much greater pain. She didn't even try to suppress her screams. Each one gave Klaus a rush that was akin to orgasm.

Sweat began to pour from his brow with the exertion, but he didn't notice. He noticed nothing but the power surging through his blood with every stroke.

After about ten blows, Sofie's screams began to subside. The pain was still excruciating, but she sank into a kind of shock. Her sight turned grey and misty as she began to lose consciousness.

Ah, blessed oblivion! God hadn't forgotten her prayer …

Klaus arm was raised to deliver another blow when the warning siren halted all movements.

Air raid.

The guards holding Sofie's arms relinquished their grip and rushed to the door. Klaus stood still poised to continue the beating.

One of the guards beckoned. "*Schnell*, Klaus! It's an air raid! Forget the Jew."

Klaus swore at the interruption of his long-awaited revenge. He looked down at Sofie's pulpy back, and the sight helped soothe his frustration.

"Next time, bitch, I will kill you," he promised.

He tossed the hose aside and wiped his forehead on his sleeve as he ran to his post.

The siren continued to wail, penetrating the periphery of Sofie's consciousness. The rat-a-tat of machine gun fire punctuated the rhythmic undulation of the siren. She struggled against the tide of blissful nothingness that would block out her pain, forcing herself to remain conscious.

The agony that shot down her spine when she tried to stand drove her to her knees, but her fear of being blown to bits, alone in this torture chamber, was greater. She had to make it back to the barracks before the siren stopped, before Klaus came back.

She didn't try again to stand upright, but crawled towards the door. Red-hot pokers of pain raced up and down her back when she tried to turn the doorknob. She collapsed against the door, unable to go on.

This is how it will end. I will die here …

The acrid odor of gun smoke assailed her nostrils. She no longer cared what happened to her. She understood the kind of freedom that accompanies apathy, and a sense of peace enveloped her.

The guns sounded farther away now ...
The grey curtain fell before her eyes and she heard nothing more.

"Grace is deceitful, and beauty is vain; But a woman that feareth the Lord, she shall be praised."

CHAPTER 14

ONE ICY MORNING IN JANUARY 1945, Sofie was awakened not by the blows of a knobby stick but by a peculiar silence more deafening than cannon fire. The sun was high up, telling Sofie that something strange was happening. In the winter months, roll call took place long before sunrise.

It had been two weeks since the day Klaus had beaten her almost to death. She realized now that the air raid had saved her, for she knew Klaus would not have put down that rubber hose until she was dead.

The surprise air raid had sufficiently disrupted camp routine that no evening roll was called that day. One of the women in her barrack had been brave enough to slip away and look for Sofie. When she found her unconscious on the floor of the punishment block, she helped her back to the barrack where they ministered to her as best they could.

Though her back still pained her, the open wounds were healing and no infection had set in, thank God. She hadn't seen Klaus since the beating, though she didn't know when he might appear again to kill her.

She now sat very still on her bunk, listening. There were no shouts from *kapos*, no moans from the dying, no cracks of the whip. She heard no barking dogs straining against their harnesses, eager to tear into flesh and bone.

The other women in the barracks were listening too. Despite their intense curiosity, no one dared venture outside. What if it was only some kind of perverse Nazi trick?

A tattoo of rapid hoofbeats broke the stillness, followed by a telltale snort. The women looked at one another in confusion. A horse was occasionally seen in the camp, usually bearing an S. S. officer who preferred not to muddy his boots. But it never galloped.

Sofie could stand it no longer. She climbed down gingerly from her bunk, feeling very fragile. She crept to the door and cracked it open to peer outside. Sunlight glittered off the icy ruts that patterned the ground, momentarily blinding her. She blinked several times until her eyes adjusted. She opened the door a bit wider and blinked again, this time in disbelief.

Not a soul was in sight. There were no S. S. with rifles and dogs, no *kapos* with raised sticks, no shouted epithets. The Nazis were gone.

If other prisoners throughout the camp had already made the same miraculous discovery, apparently they were still afraid to leave the relative safety of their barracks. A possible ambush by the Nazis was a very real fear and taking action on their own did not come easy for many. Their freedom and drive had been brutally suppressed for so long that initiative was an alien characteristic. One did not leave the barracks until ordered to do so.

Sofie was no exception. Although she had successfully evaded the annihilation planned for her, she had not been impervious to the Nazis' special mode of sub-humanization. She dared not step outside.

The hoofbeats grew louder. She could see soldiers on horseback now. Sofie quickly shut the door and hoped they had not seen her. Her heart thudded rapidly as she leaned against the door, afraid and uncertain.

A loud whoof came from the other side of the door. Someone dismounted in front of Block 18.

Pounding on the door. A voice called out in a language they didn't understand.

"*Tovarishchi! Vui svobodiy!*"

A shriek came from the bottom tier of bunks and a small woman scrambled to her feet. She was no more than 24, but her wizened appearance belied her true age. She moved very fast for one so emaciated.

Pushing Sofie aside, she tugged at the door. "He's Russian!" she half-sobbed, half-laughed. "The liberation has come!"

The door swung wide, framing a Russian officer warmly clad against the cold. His scarf covered much of his face, but his eyes took in the group of scraggly, astonished scarecrows gathered around the door.

Once again he said, "*Vui svobodiy!*"

The young woman clasped her hands together and touched her head to them in joy. She sank to her knees, sobbing. The officer bent to help her, thinking her too weak to stand. Through her tears she began babbling in Russian, her joy making her almost incoherent.

The officer took her arm and helped her to her feet, handing her over to the care of the other women. In Russian he told them, "The Germans are gone. We have liberated the camp and you are all free."

The young woman calmed down enough to translate his words into Yiddish, which most of the others could understand. The translation was lost on Sofie, who knew only a few words of Yiddish, and she cast about for someone who could tell her in Dutch or English. The news quickly was passed on in several tongues. When at last she heard in her own language that it was true, the liberation was really here, she could hardly believe it.

Jan! I'll be coming home to you.

Elation was followed by sorrow when she remembered that she would be returning home alone. How would she be able to tell Jan that every one of his daughters had perished?

The other women tentatively began to leave the barracks to see this newfound freedom for themselves. Sofie lingered by the wooden bunk where she had lived with her stepdaughters. Images flickered behind her closed eyes as she relived the demise of each one. Six young lives … six promises forever left unfulfilled. Why had she been spared and not them?

Sofie knew the question would haunt her for the rest of her life.

When the Russians rode into Auschwitz, they found only a few thousand prisoners alive. Often it was difficult to discern the living from the dead. Hardened soldiers who had weathered the war in some of the worst conditions possible cried unashamedly when they saw the walking skeletons. Medics treated the sick as best they could until the Red Cross convoys arrived. Those who were capable were free to leave whenever they wished.

Liberation did not come without bitter irony. The abrupt transition from incarceration to freedom was difficult for the prisoners to comprehend. For so long, they had been terrified even to raise their eyes from their feet, and now all of a sudden they were allowed to walk out of Auschwitz for good? This was not part of their reality. Sofie had spent countless hours fantasizing how she would react when liberation finally came. She had dreamed about running as fast as her enervated body could go, right through the archway and out of the camp, breathing deep of the smell of freedom.

Now the moment had arrived, but Sofie couldn't move. She knew the Germans were gone, that the Russians had liberated them, but she was still afraid. Did she really dare approach the perimeter fence without fearing a sharpshooter's bullet? Could she actually touch the fence and not be electrocuted? After all this time, was she really free to walk out that gate as fast or slow as she pleased, not marching in formation?

Though she didn't know it, Sofie was not alone in her trepidation. The others all felt the same way, but each was so consumed by her own fears that she failed to realize they were shared by all.

It was a somewhat dazed Sofie who wrapped a horse blanket around her shoulders. She gathered up several cans of army rations a Russian soldier had given her, and walked out of Block 18. She didn't look back.

As she neared the main gate, other prisoners who were also leaving funneled towards the archway. They drew together without thinking and passed through as a group. One man spat on the ground underneath the words *Arbeit Macht Frei* as went through the gate for the last time. No one spoke about where they were going or how they would get there. The priority was to get away from Auschwitz. The rest could be figured out later.

The band stayed together as night fell, finding shelter in an abandoned barn. Sofie sighed as she lay back on a pile of clean straw, thinking no goose-down mattress could have been more comfortable. But sleep eluded her. All that day as the group had walked together, something had bothered Sofie that she couldn't put her finger on. The haze that clouded her consciousness was slowly dissipating, the reality of liberation finally sinking in. Now she knew.

For the greatest number of the liberated Jews, there was no real joy, no lasting ecstasy in their liberation. Most had lost their homes and families, their lives irretrievably shattered. They had no home to go to, no one to hug.

They had been liberated from death, but now they had to face life.

Russell Metcalf hopped down from the jeep and arched his back. Long hours in the vehicle over rutted roads had stiffened his joints until they crackled like chestnuts in the fire as he stretched. Kilo Company had orders to transport Red Cross supplies to the displaced persons camp near Berlin, and the drive had been physically and emotionally draining. All along the roads littered with shell casings and empty ration cans, Russell's convoy encountered liberated concentration camp prisoners trying to make their way home. They walked in groups and alone, in threes and pairs. Scarecrows in rags, Russell thought.

He was haunted by the hollow look in their eyes not yet eradicated by freedom. He badly wanted to distribute some of their supplies, but Kilo Company was under strict orders not to deviate. Russell understood the reason behind the orders. It would only complicate matters if they arrived at the D.P. camp with less than their full complement of matériel. But that did little to assuage the guilt he felt at having to ignore those sunken eyes.

Russell stretched his arms overhead once more before joining his buddies already in the process of unloading the trucks. Large cartons with the familiar red cross stamped on the cardboard held C-rations, clothing, and basic medical supplies. Russell bent down to grab hold of one of the cartons but straightened abruptly as something hit him in the back with a soft thud.

"Think fast!"

A lanky private with cap askew grinned at Russell. His hand held another package of gauze bandage rolls, poised and ready to aim at his target a second time, if need be.

"Hey, Metcalf! When you're through with your calisthenics, lug those over to the Red Cross tent."

With a mock glare at his pal the comedian, Russell grasped the carton and made his way to the large tent with the red cross on a white circle dominating the front flap. He ducked under the low overhang and looked around for someone in charge. His eyes rested on a thin-looking woman bandaging a little boy's knee. Russell set his burden down and went over to her.

Touching his cap, he said, "Excuse me, ma'am. I'm with the 3rd Division unit that's brought your supplies. Where do you want us to unload them?"

Sofie looked up at the soldier who was a good decade younger than she, but as old as the ravages of war had left both of them. She gave the boy's bandage a final pat and with a smile told him to run along now. She stood up to answer the soldier.

"I'll get Miss Grayson for you. She's the supply nurse."

Russell realized his mistake and started to explain, but Sofie was already gone. "She's a tough nut. Whatever happened to those "angels of mercy" we keep reading about?"

When Miss Grayson appeared, Russell was relieved to find her every inch the warmhearted Red Cross nurse of media fame. He decided not to mention the tough cookie he'd just encountered, but once Miss Grayson finished explaining where she wanted the supplies unloaded, Russell's curiosity got the best of him.

"Pardon me for asking, ma'am, but why was the nurse in here before so angry?"

Miss Grayson looked bemused. "Nurse? There's only one other nurse here, Sergeant, and she's off duty this afternoon."

"Well, ma'am, whoever was in here left in a huff when I asked where to put the supplies."

"Oh, you must mean Mrs. Rijnfeld," she laughed. "She's tough, all right. After what she's been through, I'm amazed that she's not a pile of jelly. She lost all six of her stepchildren in Auschwitz. She had gone with them when she hadn't even been ordered to, just so they wouldn't be alone."

"You mean she's not with the Red Cross?"

"She's just a refugee, Sergeant, trying to make her way home like the rest of them."

Russell felt ashamed at his initial judgment of the woman. She had suffered through the war in a way he couldn't even imagine. No wonder she'd sounded bitchy. He had an urge to talk to her, to express his regret over her losses. Moreover, he wanted to meet someone who would sacrifice her own freedom for the sake of her stepchildren.

Russell excused himself and went to look for Sofie. He found her with her arms deep in a carton of ration cans, sorting them out. Though she had taken on some flesh since arriving at the displaced persons camp, she was still thin and gaunt, a tired droop to the shoulders clad in a faded blue blouse.

Sofie sensed a presence behind her and stopped sorting. She stood up and whirled around, hazel eyes large.

"I didn't mean to scare you, ma'am. I — I just wanted to see if there were any little extras you needed or would like. Chocolate? Chewing gum?

Sofie relaxed and reminded herself that she no longer had to fear every unfamiliar sound. She scanned the soldier's face. He looked a little scared himself. Of what?

Maybe he just wanted some companionship. Lord knows he couldn't have any prurient interest in her, in the shape she was in.

"Some chewing gum would be a treat, er — Mister — ?"

"Metcalf. Sergeant Russell Metcalf, ma'am. And you're Mrs. Rinefield," he said, pleased that he could break the ice by already knowing her name.

Sofie smiled at the mispronunciation. "Rin-feld. It's Dutch."

Russell watched as Sofie chewed animatedly on a stick of Beeman's licorice gum, smacking her lips in delight.

"Good?" he asked.

"Mmm, it's been a long time since I've had chewing gum. It seems strange to chew on something I don't have to eat. A few months ago I would have seen this gum as a meal," Sofie laughed.

Russell was surprised at such a cavalier reference to her recent situation. He'd heard from other soldiers what the concentration camps were like, what condition the surviving prisoners were in. He was amazed that this one was able to laugh about the starvation that almost did her in.

"Where are you from, Sergeant Meet-kaff?" Sofie asked.

"Please call me Russell, it's easier. I'm from Boston, Massachusetts. It's on America's east coast."

"Do you have a family?"

Russell's mouth curved in a proud smile. "I have a wonderful wife named Emily. We have a little boy — I haven't seen him in a long time."

"I'm married, too. My husband has been home in Amsterdam all this time, waiting for us." Sofie's head drooped and pain clouded her hazel eyes. "I don't know how I'm going to tell him I lost our family."

Russell leaned forward on the carton, his voice was sympathetic. "Maybe if you tell me about it first, it will help. You can try it out on me. Once you've gotten the whole story out, perhaps it won't be so difficult next time."

Sofie looked at the stranger's face, so earnest and kind. Maybe it would help to talk about it. She had pushed it all aside by throwing herself into work at the D.P. camp. But how long could she delay facing the inevitable? The girls were gone and Jan would have to be told. This American soldier, for all his weathered exterior, seemed to empathize with her, wanted to help. She had been the strong one for a long time; perhaps now was a good opportunity to relinquish the title ... at least temporarily.

Sofie took a deep breath and began. She told him about marrying a widower with six daughters and how happy they all were. She told him about the call-up notice for the girls. She told him about Westerbork. She told him about the terrible train journey to Auschwitz.

And she told him about the girls. How she had made her goal each day to keep them strong, keep them going. How, despite her efforts, one by one they grew weaker and weaker in mind and body. How she tried to prod them to stand tall during *selektions*, to raise their knees high when they jogged past *Herr Doktor* Mengele.

She told him about Lena's rape and subsequent mental breakdown.

She told him how Elli, Jopie, and Anneke were each selected for gassing when Sofie's prodding could no longer hide their weakened condition. How Carla and finally Mirjam succumbed to deadly typhus shortly before the liberation.

Russell was unaware of the tears coursing down his face. Sofie's voice remained curiously even as she told her story, but Russell felt the pain of her experience keenly. He thought of his own son and what it would be like to lose him — multiplied by six. But what amazed Russell the most was Sofie's selflessness. She accompanied her stepdaughters — who were not even her biological children — to a hellish place, with no thought for herself. How many people in this life would make such a sacrifice? Even now, she didn't spend her days giving over to grief. She assisted wherever she could in the D.P. camp: with the Red Cross, translating, minding the children.

Later, Russell would finally come to understand the source of Sofie's limitless strength of character. It was Auschwitz itself. Virtues and vices were intensified inside the concentration camps. Whoever had a warm heart when they arrived encountered every opportunity to develop it further. Whoever entered the camps proud and self-interested, left them proud and self-interested … if they left at all. Whoever remembered that the road to survival is paved with the cruelest obstacles ultimately realized that the destination is well worth the arduous journey.

It was a lesson Russell never forgot.

March 30, 1945

Dearest Em,

This will probably be my last letter to you before I'm shipped stateside. I'm not sorry; I'd rather hold you in my arms than write you letters any day! We have a few more weeks to wrap things up here and then we'll be heading for Ramstein and points west. I'm counting the days, hon!

Em, I've met the most incredible woman. She was in the D.P. camp (oops, that's "displaced persons" camp) after being liberated from Auschwitz by the Russians. She's from Holland and went to Auschwitz just so her six stepdaughters wouldn't be alone there. The horrible part is that she's the only one who made it. Now she's got to tell her husband once she gets back home. She's dreading it, but I tried to reassure her that she'd get through it. Sofie can handle just about anything, I think.

Oh, yeah — that's her name: Sofie Rijnfeld. She was able to hitch a ride with Kilo Company to the German-Dutch border. After that, she should have no trouble making her way to Amsterdam. She'll be home by now, and hopefully putting the pieces of her life back together. I gave her our address, and she promised to let me know how she's doing.

I wish you could have met her, Em. Getting to know Sofie was a part of the war I never bargained on. I don't know exactly how or why, but meeting her has changed me in some way. Maybe I'm plain nuts and it's just the war, but I feel as though nothing can ever be the same again.

Do you know what I mean?

Love you, baby --
Russ

"Many daughters have done valiantly, But thou excellest them all."

CHAPTER 15

SOFIE CLIMBED DOWN from the back of the truck and brushed the bits of dirt and hay off her clothes. She waved to the driver, thanking him for the ride.

Home. At last she was home. She looked around at the familiar streets, at the shops and houses that looked very much the same. She hugged herself in happiness.

When the American soldiers offered her a ride to the German-Dutch border, she had barely enough time to gather her things together before the convoy departed. Consequently, she had been unable to get word to Jan of her whereabouts. She knew it was probably unfair to burst in on him like this. At the same time, her mischievous side looked forward to the look on his face when he saw her.

For the moment, she forgot that she was returning alone.

She hurried up the street and turned the corner. There was her house! She ran up to the front door and smacked it several times with her open palm.

"Jan! Open up, darling! It's me!"

No answer.

Silly, she berated herself, you didn't even see if it's open.

She turned the handle. The door was unlocked. She stepped into the entry hall and listened to the stillness.

"Jan?"

No answer.

She looked around, drinking in the familiar surroundings and the utter relief at being home again. As she stood in the vestibule she recalled the long-ago day when Jopie and David became engaged. How noisy and gay it had been! Now the entry hall was quiet and forbidding.

Where could Jan be? Sofie went into the living room and walked slowly around, running her finger over the fine layer of dust that covered the carved wood frame of the sofa. She turned to head upstairs when she abruptly came face to face with a policeman. He had been silently watching her from the vestibule. Sofie let out a little shriek.

The policeman was stern. "Can I help you, *mevrouw?*"

"This is my home, constable. I've been in a D.P. camp in Germany and have come back to find my husband."

The constable took in Sofie's shabby appearance and looked skeptical. "Your home? And what is your husband's name, *mevrouw?*"

"Jan Rijnfeld."

"Ah, yes, the Rijnfelds. But this house has not belonged to them in years, *mevrouw*. It was sold after the family perished in the war."

Sofie's tone became anxious. "But I didn't perish! Our daughters did, but I've come back and I need to find my husband!"

The policeman sighed in mock patience. "*Mevrouw*, Jan Rijnfeld's body was never returned to Amsterdam. No one knows where he died."

"His body?"

The constable immediately recognized his mistake. She didn't know.

He stammered now. "*Mevrouw*, I'm — I'm sorry. I thought for certain that you knew."

"Knew what? Please, what's happened to my husband?"

Even if she wasn't Rijnfeld's wife, the woman was clearly upset. Perhaps she was a former mistress? Whoever she was, if she'd been close to Rijnfeld, she was entitled to an explanation.

"Jan Rijnfeld was rounded up during a *razzia* in '43. He was taken away with a group of other Jews. He was never heard from again."

Sofie swayed slightly, and the constable made to catch her in case she fainted. She managed not to swoon, but she paled visibly and started to shake.

Throughout all the torment she had endured, never did it once occur to her that Jan would not be there for her to come home to. That was what had kept her from giving up, even when the girls died. Perhaps it was fortunate that the idea had not crossed her mind.

Except now she was alone.

The constable's tone was more kindly now. "Is there someone you wish me to call, *mevrouw*? A friend or relative, perhaps?"

Sofie's initial shock wore off and she began to cry. "My parents live in Maarssen, but I can't leave here. I need to stay in Amsterdam and find out what happened to my husband."

It surprised the constable that Sofie wasn't curious to learn if her parents were still alive, but he said nothing. No use adding to the distraught woman's anguish.

"Come, *mevrouw*, let me take you to the Red Cross office, he urged. They can find you a place to sleep tonight, and help you locate your husband."

The constable didn't enjoy giving the woman false hopes — her husband was most certainly dead — but he felt so sorry for her, he had to say something optimistic.

Sofie allowed herself to be led away like a lost child. By now, several neighbors had gathered on the sidewalk to investigate the commotion. None had lived there before the war. None of them knew Sofie.

Tongues clucked and heads whispered together as Sofie was led away by the policeman. The Van Öys should take greater care to lock their front door, they agreed. These days, there were too many crazy people wandering the streets ...

The Amsterdam Red Cross was very solicitous of Sofie. They calmed her down, gave her a clean change of clothes, and a cot in a back room to sleep in. After she had cleaned up and eaten a hot meal, she went to bed and slept for fourteen hours. When she awoke, a pleasant looking young woman with a Red Cross armband on her sleeve stood by her cot.

She smiled at Sofie. "Are you feeling better now?" she asked gently. "You've been asleep a long time."

Sofie sat up carefully. Was it possible it had all been just a terrible nightmare?

"My husband — I need to find him."

"We want to help you, *Mevrouw* Rijnfeld. After you've freshened up, come out front and we'll talk."

Fifteen minutes later, Sofie entered the front room and smoothed her hair. She really wasn't worried how her hair looked; it was just her old nervous habit. She felt physically rested but her heart lay heavy in her chest. As much as she needed to hear the truth about Jan, she dreaded it at the same time.

The Red Cross volunteer was seated behind a desk and beckoned Sofie. She smiled, indicating the chair opposite her. Sofie perched hesitantly on the edge of the seat.

The woman reached across the desk and took hold of Sofie's hand that gripped the edge of the cold metal desk. Her eyes were full of sympathy.

"*Mevrouw* Rijnfeld, I know how difficult this must be for you."

The woman paused and Sofie sucked in her breath.

"Your husband was taken in one of the last *razzias* before the Germans pulled out of Amsterdam. We believe he was sent to Auschwitz and perished there."

Sofie could not believe what she was hearing. Jan had been in the same concentration camp, and none of them had known? Worse still, all the time that she had desperately tried to bring home as many of Jan's daughters as she could, she never once conjectured that they might return to an empty house.

It would have been better if I had died with girls, she thought miserably. One thought consoled her. At least Jan will never know that the girls didn't make it. At least he died thinking that I was there to protect them.

The guilt over her failure to keep them alive was still very much with her, but at least Jan would never know of it. For that, she was thankful.

The Red Cross verified that her parents were still alive and well, and not knowing what else to do, Sofie moved in with them. Her parents told her that the Jews of Maarssen had, for the most part, been left alone by the Nazis. Despite the Nazi directive, the Mecklenbergs had not registered with the S. S., deciding the odds were pretty good that they wouldn't be found out. Luckily, there had been no repercussions. The reasons why escaped them, but there were not about to question their good fortune.

The Mecklenbergs were thankful for Sofie's survival and were as sympathetic to their daughter as they knew how. Sofie appreciated their efforts to comfort her, but how could anyone who hadn't experienced the camps themselves understand what she had gone through, what she was still going through? She tried to describe to her parents the horrors she and the girls had endured. Though they appeared willing to listen, Sofie saw the look in their eyes that belied their empathetic demeanor. It wasn't long before Papa began changing the subject whenever she spoke of Auschwitz. Their inability to face the reality of Sofie's experiences increased her sense of isolation.

She was truly alone.

One afternoon, the doorbell rang as Sofie was just hanging up her apron after drying the dishes from their meager meal of boiled potatoes. She heard Papa get up from the living room sofa to answer it. She listened, straining to hear who it was. When all she heard was an odd silence, she went to see for herself who had come to call.

Papa stood with the newspaper still folded in his hand. He seemed at a loss for words. Sofie looked toward the tall figure standing in the front hall.

"David!" she squealed, flinging herself into his arms with girlish abandon, almost knocking him over in the process. "How did you find me? How are your parents?" A hundred questions welled up inside Sofie who was overjoyed to see him.

David Davidson gently extracted Sofie's arms from around his neck. He took a step back but didn't let go of her hands. He was equally elated to find her. Sofie was his last remaining link to Jopie.

Sofie's joy in seeing David eclipsed all else in that moment. Grateful though she was that her parents had escaped persecution, the realization that they were the only family she had left was hard to accept. There were times lately when she wondered if those few years of happiness with Jan and the girls had been an elaborate dream from which she was just now waking. Her parents tried to be comforting but were helpless to understand the depth of her loss and the circumstances surrounding it. For them, it was enough that their daughter had survived and come back to them, where she obviously belonged.

Standing with David in the front hall of her parents' home, Sofie felt more alive than she had in months. Here was someone with whom she could recall the laughter, the love they had shared with the Jan Rijnfeld family.

Oh, God — David didn't know yet about Jopie. Sofie turned cold at the prospect of telling David that his fianceé was gone. Then she realized that she and David shared the same grief. Perhaps they could help each other the way no one else could.

She drew him into the living room. "Come sit, David," she said. "There is much I have to tell you."

"Give her of the fruit of her hands;
And let her works
praise her in the gates."

CHAPTER 16

London   *May 10, 1947*

Dear Russell,

I finally received your letter and the photos you sent. The postmark was a month old, so it must have gotten lost somewhere along the way. It was wonderful to hear from you, and the family photo brought Emily, Peter, and little Susie to life for me. I feel like I already know them.

As you can see by the return address, I now live in England. After David and I married, we thought it best to leave Holland altogether. It wasn't so much that we wanted to leave the past behind, but we felt it was important to start our future elsewhere. We encountered a good deal of opposition to our marriage from David's family and many people we had once thought were good friends.

I'm not sure what bothered people most: the fact that David had been engaged to my stepdaughter, or the 15-year difference in our ages. We finally tired of the gossip and decided to make a new life. My cousin Gerda lives here in London, so this is where we ended up. She's been wonderful. She sponsored our immigration, and put us up until we could find our own place. We're settling into our new home nicely.

I know it's difficult for most people to understand, but marrying David has been *healing, for both of us. We grieve together, but we now smile together too. We smile at the same memories we share of a beautiful girl we both loved, and at the memories we hope to create together. Maybe we'll even visit America one day. I do so want to meet Emily and the children.*

Keep well, my friend, and write soon.

Always,
Soof

Emily Metcalf bounced the baby on her hip, trying to quiet her. Susie was cutting a tooth and had been very fussy of late. Two year old Peter sat on the kitchen floor with his new set of Lincoln Logs, intent on the house he was building.

Emily walked back and forth with the baby and looked over at Russell. He was sitting at the kitchen table with that faraway look in his eyes again. It was a look she had come to know well. It always came over him after reading a letter from the Dutch woman he'd met during the war.

It wasn't that Emily was jealous of — what was the nickname Russell used? — Soof. Russell had told Emily enough about the woman for her to understand that their relationship was purely platonic. It was just that she felt so left out. Whenever one of Soof's letters arrived, it was as though Russell was transported back to Europe, back to a part of his life Emily couldn't share.

Russell knew that Em resented the correspondence he maintained with his friend. He'd hidden nothing from his wife, told her right from the start that there was nothing romantic between him and Soof. He'd told Emily about Sofie's family and the sacrifice she had made in going with them to Auschwitz. He'd told her how he admired Sofie's courage after she'd seen her daughters removed, one by one, to be killed. Emily was fascinated by the stories Russell told of this woman, and appreciated how he could be so taken with her.

But Russell doubted that Emily fully comprehended what drew him and Sofie together, how their lives were linked. Only someone who had

154

been there, who had seen the horrors of the war, could truly understand how life can never be the same again.

The baby began to whimper. Emily sighed and shifted Susie to her other hip. It was useless right now to try permeating the bubble that encased her husband. From experience, she knew if she was patient, the bubble would eventually thin out until it disappeared. Then she would have her Russell back.

Until Sofie's next letter, that is …

For Sofie and David Davidson, postwar Holland had held little more for them than sadness and judgment. The war had taken from them the people they loved most, but in each other they were able to reconstruct a modicum of that love. Their common grief proved to be a balm to their empty hearts. Though they didn't plan it that way, their fondness for each other soon grew beyond their mutual connection to Jopie.

After their marriage, Sofie's cousin Gerda sponsored their immigration to England and had been very helpful in getting them resettled. They found a charming flat in a residential neighborhood that fell within their budget. Gerda helped David obtain a position with a prominent London furrier, who had been more than happy to take on a young man with generations of experience in the trade.

The 15 year gap in their ages didn't cause the double takes and whispers that it had in Holland. Perhaps this was partly due to the fact that the war had taken its toll on David s appearance. Grief had etched its mark on his face, making him appear older than he was. Sofie's weight loss from her time in the camps now presented a more youthful demeanor than she'd had as a plump matron.

Neither Sofie nor David questioned the fates that had brought them together. They had been given a second chance at love and were not about to wonder how or why. As far as Mr. and Mrs. David Davidson were concerned, their marriage was proof that whenever God closes a door, somewhere he opens a window.

Sofie hopped down from the double-decker bus and blinked into the sunshine glaring off the broad windshield. It was a beautiful afternoon in late April, the time of year for new beginnings. Sofie checked the address on the piece of paper in her hand and walked one block east to the Knightsbridge Professional Building. She entered the hushed lobby, high heels clicking loudly on the polished floor. She took the elevator to the fourth floor and the office of Dr. Alfred Brinsley, Practise of Dermatology. After giving her name to the receptionist, she took a seat in the spartan waiting room, perching on the edge of the chair in her anxious way.

Ever since the day she received it, Sofie had always known she would someday have her tattoo removed, that grisly souvenir from Auschwitz she had dangerously contrived to have made smaller than usual. She ran her finger thoughtfully over the blurred numbers on her arm. Everyone at Auschwitz who knew the story had thought she was crazy to risk bribing the tattooist to make small numbers. But Sofie had known even then — just as she had known she would survive — that her plan would be realized.

The receptionist ushered Sofie into Dr. Brinsley's private office and indicated a chair opposite the doctor's desk. The office was small but neat, with paneled walls and a built-in bookcase. A desk clock ticked reassuringly, its small pendulum ceaselessly swinging.

The door opened and a pleasant-looking man in his late thirties came in. He smiled at Sofie and introduced himself as Alfred Brinsley. He had a thick crop of prematurely silver hair and a tailored suit that looked expensive.

"How do you do, Mrs. Davidson," he asked kindly, "What brings you here today?"

Sofie got right to the point. She placed her forearm on the doctor's desk, the tattoo facing up and clearly visible. "This," she answered simply.

Dr. Brinsley met her eyes briefly before he bent to look at Sofie's arm. His brows came together as he examined the tattoo.

"How much would it cost to have it removed, Doctor?" Sofie asked.

"The procedure itself is uncomplicated, Mrs. Davidson. A simple excision of the layer of skin penetrated by the ink. Then there's the anaesthetic, sutures, dressings …"

Dr. Brinsley's voice trailed off and he leaned back in his chair. "I'm curious about something, Mrs. Davidson. I've seen these tattoos before, but never one so small in area. Is there any significance to the difference in size?"

"I've never been a vain woman, Dr. Brinsley, but this is one aspect of my appearance I definitely want to change. I decided that the day I received this little memento. I figured that the smaller the tattoo, the easier it would be to remove. So I bribed the *kapo* to make the numbers smaller."

Dr. Brinsley was intrigued. "But what could you use for bribes? I understood that the S. S. confiscated all belongings and were very thorough in their searches for contraband."

To her own surprise, Sofie felt her cheeks grow hot. "I was able to smuggle in a gold watch," she murmured and looked away.

Dr. Brinsley was not insensitive to Sofie's discomfiture. He had apparently hit a raw nerve with his question. Although he was curious to know how she had managed to smuggle in jewelry, he wasn't going to be a boor and press the issue. Mrs. Davidson was a woman with a strong personality, but she also wore a patina of vulnerability.

Admittedly, he had been somewhat surprised when he saw the telltale numbers on her arm. The concentration camp survivors he had seen wore their past on their faces and in their eyes. But when he entered his office and saw Mrs. Davidson, there were no revealing signs that identified her as a camp survivor. No haunted look behind the hazel eyes, no furrows of pain and loss etched into her face. She wore a pleasant smile. Only now that he knew the reason for her visit did he detect the slightest sadness behind the ruby-tinted lips.

Sofie pretended to be interested in the books lining the walnut shelves in the wall, still unable to meet the doctor's eyes.

Dr. Brinsley cleared this throat. "Enough said, Mrs. Davidson. I know what the tattoo signifies and what you've been through. Let's set up an appointment for Thursday. The excision can be done here in the office; a hospital stay isn't necessary."

"And the cost?" Sofie asked, "My husband is just getting started, you see, and — "

"There will be no charge, Mrs. Davidson. You've already paid your dues ... and then some."

Sofie decided to walk home instead of taking the bus. It was such a beautiful day, and she wanted some time to think about her visit with

Dr. Brinsley, to sort out her confused feelings. She wondered about the doctor's strange albeit generous offer. Why was he doing it?

She gave herself a mental shake. What was wrong with her? Dr. Brinsley was merely a kind man performing a *mitzvah*. When had she become so suspicious of generosity?

And this business of blushing and stammering over her smuggled watch … such behavior was completely alien to Sofie. She had always been so sure of herself, so realistic. Now she was acting like a shrinking violet over something that had been a necessary evil. True, it wasn't something you'd chat about over tea, but the doctor had asked. Surely he was acquainted with some of the nightmare stories of the war …

Sofie walked along, lost in her own thoughts, oblivious to the glories of the season surrounding her. She had walked nine city blocks but was no closer to understanding these strange emotions that enveloped her.

A car horn startled her out of her reverie. She looked around to get her bearings and realized she was not far from Dickerson's Furs. On an impulse, she decided to stop in and see David. Her feet were starting to hurt a little, anyway. She should have known better than to walk so far in platforms.

The shop manager greeted her. "Ah, Mrs. Davidson. How delightful to see you."

"Thank you, Mr. Price. I just popped in to see David. Is he busy?"

"Not too busy to say hello to his wife, I should imagine. Do come in." Mr. Price held aside the velvet curtain that separated the front of the store from the back room.

David looked up from the inventory report he was working on and smiled at Sofie.

"Hi, darling. What a nice surprise." He kissed her cheek. The front door chimed and Mr. Price excused himself to wait on the customer.

"What's up, Soof?" David asked, "How did your appointment go?"

"It was fine. The doctor said he can remove the tattoo very easily."

"Is this Brinsley fellow a decent sort?"

Sofie smiled. "You might say that. He's going to remove it for nothing."

David's reaction was not the one Sofie expected. She thought he would be pleased and touched at the doctor's benevolence, but instead he became indignant.

"Wait a minute, now. Does he think we're just poor war refugees who need his charity?"

"David, don't be like that. I think Dr. Brinsley is making a beautiful gesture. He said he knew what the tattoo means, and that I've already paid my dues."

David's expression softened. Sofie felt relieved at the return of his usual easygoing manner. Apparently she wasn't the only one who was experiencing uncharacteristic moods today.

"David. There's something I want to talk to you about." She took his hand. "I think it's time we started thinking about becoming a real family."

"You mean have a baby?"

"Yes, *schatje*. There's nothing I'd like more. I think it would be the best thing for us." She held her breath, waiting for his response.

David took his wife in his arms. "Oh, Soof, it's what I want, too. I was afraid that after losing all the girls, you wouldn't want to start over again."

Sofie disengaged herself and searched his face with misty eyes. "I have started over, David. You and I have started a new life together. But I was so afraid you would be against the idea."

"Against having children of my own? Of our own? Not on your life!" He embraced her again.

David felt Sofie's tears against his shoulder and he held her closer, awash in a feeling of tenderness. Perhaps Sofie's calling in life was putting together families like jigsaw puzzles, he mused. She took disjointed pieces and worked with them until they fit just right, completing a picture that hadn't been there before. David had seen first-hand the happiness Sofie had brought to the Rijnfeld family. This time, he looked forward to being part and parcel of the magic Sofie would weave in creating the Davidson family.

Sofie's face grew serious. "David, this is one instance where we have to consider our ages. I'm not a young woman anymore. There might be complications — and the possibility of birth defects are that much greater."

David looked at the hazel eyes now clouded simultaneously with doubt and hope. "We owe it to ourselves to try, Soof. And we owe it to

Jopie, Jan, and the rest. Life must go on, you know. Our child is their legacy."

Sofie brought his hand to her cheek. "Thank you, darling," she said simply.

The couple girded themselves with patience, positive that conception would not happen immediately. But to their surprise, Sofie found herself pregnant two months later. She was elated, and David's deep joy at the news made her own happiness complete. They would lie awake at night, touching her not-yet-growing belly and discuss names for the child. Both agreed that, if it was a girl, she would be called Jopie.

The question of a boy's name raised controversy, however. If they had a son, Sofie felt he should be named for David's father, who had died of a heart attack just after their marriage. David flatly refused, maintaining that "Hans" sounded "too German."

"But it's Jewish tradition," Sofie argued. "A child is named for a deceased relative, usually a grandparent or great-grandparent."

David was adamant. No son of his would go through life with such an obviously German name. Not after what they had suffered at the hands of the Germans.

Sofie didn't press the issue, seeing she would get nowhere with David this night. It was late and they both were tired. Besides, she didn't want to spoil the intimacy of the moment with an argument. They had all the time in the world ...

"She considereth a field, and buyeth it; With the fruit of her hands she planteth a vineyard."

CHAPTER 17

AS IT TURNED OUT, Sofie and David never got around to deciding the question of their son's name. When she was four months pregnant, Sofie miscarried. It happened so suddenly and innocuously that she couldn't believe it really happened. She had thought miscarriage meant writhing pains and hemorrhaging. Sofie had only some mild abdominal cramping that sent her to the loo, where she quietly lost their baby.

David was inconsolable. Hadn't they had enough loss? Were loved ones always going to be taken from them?

Once again, Sofie found solace in comforting others. She held David tightly as he grieved and wondered why she wasn't just as emotional. She had wanted this baby as much as David, maybe more. Why wasn't she sobbing her heart out over yet another child lost to her?

The answer was visible, if one looked closely enough. Just after Sofie learned of Jan's death, an invisible sheath had crept in like an insidious parasite, quietly and unobtrusively enveloping her heart. The sheath was impervious to all but the sharpest of sorrows that sought to pierce it. While it armored Sofie against unendurable heartbreak, it also precluded her from experiencing the fullness of true joy. Her pregnancy had been so short-lived that Sofie never had a chance for acceptance to work its way through the sheath and allow her to revel in the miracle of it. The whole thing now seemed only a dream. Perhaps more vivid than most, but a dream, nonetheless.

After a few months, David and Sofie decided to try again. They were still determined to have their family, and one miscarriage did not extinguish their hopes. It took a year this time, but the following summer Sofie was pregnant again. They were just as excited this time, if not a trifle more guarded. By unspoken agreement, they didn't indulge themselves in pillow talk about names and genders. Sofie was content to pat her belly and smile to herself, while David never failed to press his lips to her swelling abdomen after first kissing Sofie good-night. When she approached the end of her fourth month, she and David relaxed a little, feeling that the danger was past. They even laughed a little over their cautious attitude.

They were right to have been cautious. Sofie was awakened one morning in her fifth month by sharp pains cutting through her middle. She threw back the covers and sat on the edge of the bed, waiting. After a few minutes, she rose carefully and headed for the bathroom. A cramp, sharper than before, stabbed her middle. She tried not to cry out, but a moan did escape her lips, waking David, who immediately ran to the phone.

The ambulance was there within ten minutes. Through her pain, Sofie's thoughts were clear and she understood the meaning of it all. She thought ruefully that this time God must have wanted to make sure she got the message, loud and clear. The baby had been real, but apparently not hers to keep.

David came to the hospital every day, always carrying a single red rose that he placed in a bud vase on the table by her bed. His reaction to the second miscarriage was much more composed, almost resigned. Sofie was grateful, for this loss hit her much harder emotionally than before, and she didn't feel quite the usual Pillar of Strength.

Within a week, Sofie was much stronger physically. David sat on the bed, helping Sofie get dressed to leave the hospital. Her movements were slow, but she refused his helping hands, insisting that she felt perfectly fine. Just before they were ready to leave, Dr. Waybury came in.

"All ready to go, I see!" he said cheerfully.

David returned the smile, but Sofie dully answered, "Yes."

Dr. Waybury looked sympathetically at the couple. This was one part of his job he detested. "Sofie, David, I'm going to be frank with you. The odds of carrying a child to term are not good."

Sofie glanced at David's downcast expression and immediately acknowledged her own inadequacy. She should never have saddled him with an older woman for a wife, one that couldn't have children.

Dr. Waybury continued, "Sofie's uterine lining is very thin. The embryo cannot attach itself securely, resulting in spontaneous abortion."

The Davidsons were silent. Dr. Waybury handed David a slip of paper. David read the name and number on it and looked at the doctor questioningly.

"Mrs. Fretwell is a patient of mine. I've taken the liberty of arranging an appointment for you at her office tomorrow. One o'clock," Dr. Waybury said.

He shook David's hand and squeezed Sofie's shoulder in consolation. "Good luck. Call me if you need anything."

After he left, David handed Sofie the slip of paper. She unfolded it and read, *Dorothy Fretwell, Greater London Children's Services, tel. 022-363*.

Much to Dr. Waybury's surprise, the meeting he'd arranged between the Davidsons and Greater London Children's Services did not go smoothly. He'd taken a personal interest in the Davidsons' history and was saddened by their inability to have a child. The week after Sofie had been discharged from the hospital, Dr. Waybury phoned the agency and asked to speak to Mrs. Fretwell.

Dorothy Fretwell was a prim woman in her early thirties. She had shining blonde hair and attractive features, but her severe attire and face bare of makeup quelled any potential beauty. When she spoke, her tone was clipped, professional.

"Dr. Waybury, how nice to hear from you ... Ah, yes, Mr. and Mrs. Davidson. A most interesting couple ... yes, they're fine people, I'm sure, but I'm afraid they don't qualify as adoption candidates here at GLCS ... No ... no, it's not their age difference — though I must say I do find that a trifle unusual — no, it was their background, I'm afraid. I believe Mr. Davidson had been engaged to his wife's stepdaughter … yes, Doctor, I'm aware that she died in a concentration camp, poor soul. But this sort of affinity is rather, er … unconventional … No, I'm afraid that would be quite impossible. Mrs. Davidson experienced years of trauma during the war, and we just can't be certain how that will affect her emotional stability in the future … No, I doubt that would do any good. Rules are rules. But thank you for referring them to me, Doctor. So good of you to call … "

Sofie and David refused to give up. They went from one agency to another, only to be turned down every time. Either Sofie was too old, their relationship was too idiosyncratic, or … There was always some reason why they were deemed unsuitable. Not once did they hear any words of encouragement, any validation that their loving home would be a blessing for any child.

The repeated rejections soon took their toll on David. After two years of hoping against hope, rallying from disappointment only to have their hopes dashed yet again, he'd had enough.

"Soof, I'm sorry, but I just can't do this anymore. Maybe we're just not meant to have children."

"*Schatje*, please don't give up yet. Besides, we have that appointment tomorrow. It's all set," Sofie pleaded.

"How many more times do you want to get hurt, Soof? How many times do you have to be turned away before you accept the fact that no agency will consider us?"

"However many times it takes, David," she said quietly. "I'm not giving up. Somewhere out there is a child who needs us as much as we need her. And I'm not giving up until I find her."

Sofie spent the next month researching more orphanages and putting out feelers to anyone and everyone who might lead her to the child she wanted so desperately. David was certain her hopes would only be crushed again, but he kept this to himself. Some things Soof had to learn for herself, however painful it might be.

Her persistence paid off. Sofie's networking led them to the War Orphans' Home, a large, poorly-funded facility that housed over 200 European children orphaned by the war. When the Davidsons toured the

Home for the first time, Sofie was taken aback by the shabby condition of the two great buildings that comprised the orphanage. Paint was peeling in many places, light was dim from many burned-out bulbs, and the only floor covering to be seen was in the director's office. There was, Sofie was relieved to see, an extensive playground equipped with sandboxes and swings, all homemade by charitable friends of the staff.

Sofie and David were ushered into the office of the director, Cecily Langton.

"Do sit down, Mr. and Mrs. Davidson. I'm sorry I can't offer you any refreshment, but as you can see, our resources here are somewhat limited," Mrs. Langton apologized.

"Please don't worry," David assured her, "We're fine."

Mrs. Langton removed her harlequin glasses and smiled. "I'm awfully glad you're interested in adopting. We have so many needy children here, and most couples prefer to adopt infants."

She shuffled some papers and took up a pencil. "We just have a few formalities to dispense with here. Red tape, you know." She replaced her glasses and poised her pencil over the sheet in front of her. "Now, if you will give me your ages, please."

Sofie and David exchanged looks. Here it comes …

David tried to answer casually. "I'm 31, and my wife is 46." They braced themselves for the usual shocked reaction.

Mrs. Langton noted their ages on the form without comment. "And do you have any biological children?"

Sofie and David were so surprised at the director's matter-of-fact acceptance that they couldn't find their voices. During interviews at other adoption agencies, it was at this point that the director would cap her pen, shake hands with them politely, and thank them for coming down. For the first time in their quest, their ages were not an issue. If Mrs. Langton took note of the fact that David was 15 years Sofie's junior, apparently it made no difference.

The rest of the forms were completed in short order and again Mrs. Langton removed her glasses.

"Now, Mr. and Mrs. Davidson, I'd like to discuss what sort of child you would be interested in."

Sofie and David absorbed this. They had a choice?

Mrs. Langton went on, "You'll find we have all ages, genders, and backgrounds here. Some do not speak English. It helps in the process if you can state as clearly as possible what you are looking for."

Sofie spoke up without hesitation. "We want the child nobody else wants."

David looked at her in surprise. She'd never said as much to him before.

Sofie was surprised herself. She hadn't planned to say that. In fact, she had no idea where the thought came from. It just popped into her mind like the proverbial light bulb over her head. Without a second thought, she knew she had said the right thing.

"Yes, we'd like the child who is least likely to be adopted," Sofie repeated, more declarative this time.

"Soof ... " David murmured, a little hurt by her unilateral decision.

"Oh, David, I'm sorry, I know we haven't talked about this ... I didn't realize it myself until just now. We both know what it's like to be rejected, don't we? If we're going to give a child — and ourselves — a second chance at happiness, then let's give it to the child who needs it the most."

Mrs. Langton smiled at Sofie. She turned to David and said, "Your wife has a very compassionate nature, Mr. Davidson."

David's smile was tight. He was accustomed to Sofie's take-charge personality, but he bristled at this authoritarian display. Adoption was supposed to be a joint decision, a joint venture. If Sofie had a revelation that was important to her, she should be telling her husband first, not some social worker. He felt unmanned, more child himself than husband.

Sofie read the expression on David's face with concern. She could see he was having a serious mental debate. "David?"

David turned to her hopeful countenance and saw the plea in her eyes. His annoyance immediately ebbed. Sofie may be overly headstrong sometimes, but Mrs. Langton was right: she did have unusual compassion. If it was this important to her ...

David smiled. "She does indeed, Mrs. Langton. More than you know," he answered.

Sofie s face radiated happiness. She knew David had let her have her way, and she was truly appreciative.

Mrs. Langton led them out to the playground where the children were happily enjoying afternoon recess. Sofie scanned the multitude of tousled heads, hair of every color falling over faces that ranged from the palest of fair skins to dark Mediterranean complexions. Her eyes came to rest on a little girl who crouched alone in a corner by the school building. About five years old, she had lank, mouse-brown hair that fell forward as she drew lines in the dirt with a stick. She made no attempt to join the other children in their games, and they ignored her like she wasn't even there.

Mrs. Langton observed Sofie's interest and followed the direction of her gaze. Somehow she had known Mrs. Davidson would find this one. She touched Sofie's arm and held her own out to the side in a gesture of invitation.

At the approach of the strangers, the little girl looked up from her dirt drawings. Sofie stifled a gasp as she took in the distorted features, the result of an operation to correct a harelip. The deformity had been so severe that even plastic surgery could not restore her face completely.

Very gently, Sofie crouched down to the girl's level. She smiled at her and reached out to tuck the child's wayward locks behind her ear. The little girl shrank from Sofie's touch. Undaunted, Sofie held out her hand, palm-up, in a mute request for the stick the girl was using as a drawing instrument. The child hesitated, then put the stick in Sofie's hand. Sofie thanked her and began her own dirt drawing, a simple square house. She was not surprised by the little girl's uncertainty; she could imagine what the poor thing had endured during the war. She wondered what had happened to the girl's parents.

When the house was finished, Sofie handed the stick back to the child, who accepted it warily, eyeing this funny lady with suspicion. None of the grown-ups here had ever asked to draw with her before.

Sofie smiled again and pointed to the crude canvas. The little girl looked at the lone house Sofie had drawn in the dirt. With her stick she began to add to the picture, drawing a tree next to the house. Then she added some flowers. She regarded the scene critically and smiled, liking what she saw. She gave Sofie the stick, indicating that it was her turn to draw something.

David took one look at his wife's glowing face as she drew a picture of a cat, her head bent close to the little girl. They already looked like they belonged together.

He turned to Mrs. Langton. "How soon can we arrange to bring her home?"

Over David's protests, Sofie named the little girl Esther.

"But why, Soof?" David asked. "I thought we agreed we would name a daughter after Jopie."

Sofie sighed in exaggerated patience. "We've been all over this, David. Jopie will always live on in our hearts because she has us to remember her."

"Tradition says that you name your children after their forebears. It makes no sense to name our little girl after some woman you met in Westerbork! I don't mean to sound callous, Soof, but I'm sure Esther has her own relatives to preserve her memory."

"We don't know that. For all we know, her entire family might have perished."

David pressed his clenched fists to either side of his head in supreme frustration. When Sofie made up her mind about something, there was no discussion. He wondered fleetingly why Jopie had never made mention of this aspect of her stepmother's personality.

Sofie knew David was exasperated with her, but on this subject she was adamant. The memory of the woman who had been on the same train to Westerbork with them and whose bunk was next to hers in Barrack B was still very much with Sofie. The reedy sound of Esther's voice in prayer still haunted her consciousness. Despite Esther's pessimism about their fate, Sofie had felt sorry for her, sorry that her spirit had been beaten down so early in the game. She had a strong feeling that Esther didn't have much family to speak of, though she couldn't name the reason. It bothered her that there might never be any lasting evidence that this human being had lived and died.

Sofie looked over at her new daughter playing quietly in the corner with her doll. Until now, this little girl had been left without any family. Perhaps it was all the more fitting that the Esther of Sofie's memory found immortality in the creation of this new family.

"She is like the merchant ships; She bringeth her food from afar."

CHAPTER 18

THE POST-WAR YEARS EBBED into a new decade, one that was relatively peaceful for the Davidsons. As time went on, Esther Davidson grew into a happy, well-adjusted child who blossomed in the wealth of her adopted parents' devotion. She showed a hunger for learning that Sofie and David found astonishing in view of the near-catatonic state in which they had first met her.

It was 1960 now, and Esther had been granted a full scholarship to Jackson College in the United States. Her parents couldn't have been more proud, yet Massachusetts was so far away! England had many fine colleges, but Sofie and David knew that this was an opportunity Esther should not pass up. Off to Jackson she would go, and Sofie would have been much more trepidatious about the idea if it weren't for the letter she'd received just this morning:

> *... of course I'll watch out for Esther.*
> *I know you'd do the same for me if*
> *Susie were coming to England to attend*
> *school. So don't worry, Soof. Emily and*
> *I will take good care of her ...*

The correspondence between Sofie and Russell Metcalf had continued steadily through the years. They had not seen each other since the day Russell left Europe with his battalion, but their special friendship was cemented in the letters they exchanged faithfully. Sofie felt as though she knew Emily and the children, Peter and Susie, just as Russell was eager to meet the Esther he had heard so much about.

Yes, Sofie felt much better about her daughter going to school so far away, as long as Russell was near. He was *mishpocha*.

For the Metcalfs, life after the war had not been so easy. It had taken some time for Russell to re-acclimate himself to civilian life. No one comes home from war emotionally unscathed, but he felt as if he had to get to know Emily all over again. And the children — he'd missed so much of their development.

It took patience on everyone's part, but eventually Russell became more at ease in his own home. He even enjoyed becoming reacquainted with his wife, almost like a second honeymoon … when he wasn't playing catch with Peter or having a pretend tea party with Susie. No sooner had they all readjusted to the aftermath of World War II when the army called Russell back to active duty. It seems there was some sort of conflict over in Korea …

Once more, Emily assumed the role of caretaker of home and hearth, punctuated with the constant worry over her husband's welfare. He had come through WWII in one piece; what if his luck ran out this time? She shuddered each time the thought crossed her mind. She had two young children — how would she make it on her own, if it came to that?

When such dark musings intruded too pervasively, Emily forced herself to shake them off. She told herself firmly that Russell would come home again.

She also wondered dryly what poor lost soul he might befriend this time …

Emily knew such uncharitable thoughts would not earn her any bonus points when praying for Russell's safety. Try as she might, though, she could never shake off the resentment she harbored toward Russell's ongoing friendship with that Dutch woman. She didn't understand what bonded them together, and, despite fifteen years of marriage, she was embarrassed to be so jealous of someone she had never even met.

When the Korean Conflict ended and Russell returned safely to his family, Emily felt guilty for her previous thoughts. To her relief, Russell brought home no tales of stalwart civilians, but he was not the same man she had sent off to yet another war. She might have chalked it up to another case of post-war familial awkwardness, but it was different this time. Russell was distant and uncommunicative. Emily never asked whether he had written to Sofie from Korea (perhaps because she didn't want to know the answer?), but she doubted that a front-line soldier would have sufficient spare time to write to his family and a "pen pal."

Let's face it, Emily sighed to herself, you're jealous of Sofie. You're also too intelligent to believe that there is anything really going on between them, so snap out of it! You can't share everything with Russell, much as you'd like to. So forget this nonsense and concentrate on how to get through to your husband!

In the years that followed, Emily often repeated that little lecture to herself. It helped that, as Peter and Susie grew older, their activities kept her increasingly busy. Whenever a letter with a London postmark arrived for Russell, she immediately quashed any resentment that threatened to bubble to the surface. She convinced herself — or tried to — that she was genuinely glad when Sofie's letters came, for they lit up Russell's face and brought him out of his shell. He shared the letters with his family and explained to the children who Sofie was, now that they were old enough to understand. Peter and Susie enjoyed the letters from far away, and even they began referring to Sofie as "Tante Soof," employing the European term for "aunt." Russell joked with them about his correspondence with "Tante Soof," calling it his "Hallmark card friendship."

"What does that mean, Dad?" Peter inquired.

"Because it's across the miles, " Russell quipped.

The spoof on the trite greeting card slogan went over the children's heads, but Emily chuckled, pleased to see Russell so lighthearted. Perhaps she'd been wrong to think of Sofie as an intruder. Lately it seemed she did more good for their family than she could possibly realize.

True to his word, Russell did keep an eye out for Esther Davidson, meeting her train when it came in from New York and helping her settle into her dormitory at Jackson College in Medford. She was a tall young woman with feathery brown hair and horn-rimmed glasses framing brown eyes. Despite plastic surgery, her mouth was somewhat misshapen from the cleft lip and palate, but it was less noticeable now that she was grown. She had the aura of an intellectual, and it wasn't just the eyeglasses. When she spoke, her voice was pleasant and self-assured. Russell was amused by the clipped British tones of her speech. Sofie's heavy Dutch accent was clear in his memory, and subconsciously he had expected her daughter to talk the same way, for all that she had been reared in England.

When Russell approached Emily about having Esther to dinner, she agreed happily. She wanted very much to meet this girl and hopefully learn something of the connection between her mother and Russell.

Emily prepared a special meal of roast beef, baked potatoes, and fresh peas — what she thought of as typical English fare. She made sure Peter wore a clean shirt and tie, and starched Susie's pink organdie. She inspected the children as they stood before her, nodding approval at Peter's wet-combed hair and Susie's shiny patent leather shoes. Giving the dining room table a final check, she examined the overall effect for a long moment, then rearranged an errant leaf in the centerpiece.

Russell came up behind her and affectionately squeezed her shoulders, causing Emily to jump in surprise.

"Easy there, Em. You're so nervous!" Russell smiled.

"I just want everything to be perfect. Esther's a long way from home and on her own for the first time. I want her to feel at ease here."

Russell cocked an eye at his wife. "Are you sure you don't just want to make a good impression because you think Esther will report everything back to Soof?"

"Don't be silly, Russ," Emily said quickly, but she felt her face redden at his unexpected intuition.

The doorbell rang.

"She's here!" Russell called out.

Emily positioned Peter and Susie to one side of the foyer and took her place beside them. She was still somewhat flustered from Russell's unprecedented observation. When had he become so insightful?

Russell opened the door to a smiling Esther. She had refused Russell's offer to pick her up at the dorm, and took a taxi instead. It made her feel more independent, she had told him. Russell knew who she got that from …

Russell made the introductions and Emily greeted Esther warmly. Susie was bashful and Peter sullen because of the hated starched collar and tie. But Esther's easy manner soon won them over. By the time dessert was served, she had them enthralled with her account of the coronation of Queen Elizabeth II eight years before.

Esther was relaxed and having a good time. She appreciated the *hamish* atmosphere, as well as the delicious food.

"The food at school is bloody awful!" she told them.

Russell plied her with questions about her parents, stimulating Emily's interest. This was what she'd been waiting for …

But the tidbits of news that Esther provided failed to satisfy Emily's curiosity. Then an idea came to her.

"Do you have any photos of your parents, Esther? I'd love to see them," she asked.

"Good idea, Em," Russell added, "I've never seen Soof's husband."

Esther obligingly brought out a snapshot from her purse. The photo was passed around the table while Emily struggled to remain patient until Peter finally passed it to her. She frowned slightly at her son, who had passed the snapshot directly to her without giving it even a polite glimpse, having little interest in pictures of strangers.

She looked at the couple in the photograph and was surprised to see a nice-looking man in his early forties and a rotund woman in a dress patterned so brightly it bordered on flamboyant. This is the Soof she'd been hearing about all these years?

Russell was saying, "She looks a lot healthier than the first time I met her."

Esther laughed. "Mum has always been a large woman. She says that Auschwitz was the only diet that ever worked for her."

Emily joined the laughter that went around the table, but privately she wondered how Sofie could make jokes about a situation that almost killed her. The same thought had occurred to Russell the day he met Sofie.

Russell provided the answer. "That's your mother, Esther. Her positive attitude is what got her through. We could all take a leaf from her book."

Esther nodded in agreement. "Mum's one of the strongest people I know. She's been like that as long as I can remember. If it weren't for her optimism, I think I would have been a lot more self-conscious about my face."

Esther's reference to her slight disfigurement attracted the children's attention, and Emily saw them staring. She caught Peter's eye and shook her head "no" almost imperceptibly. He got the message and dutifully nudged his sister with his elbow.

Esther caught the exchange and sought to break the awkwardness of the moment. "It's quite all right, Mrs. Metcalf. They're bound to be curious. It's not the first time I've gotten stares."

She smiled at the children and briefly explained to them about the cleft lip and palate. "Now that you know and it's all out in the open, we needn't ever feel embarrassed, right?"

Emily was impressed with the way Esther handled the situation. It was obvious she'd received a great deal of loving support at the hands of her parents.

Suddenly Emily knew all she needed to about Sofie Davidson. There was nothing more between her and Russell than mutual respect. And if their friendship took away more of Russell than Emily would have liked, well … who was she to choose his friends?

As far as Sofie herself, after what that woman must have gone through, Emily didn't blame Russell for admiring her. As a matter of fact, Emily was starting to admire her, too.

"She is like the merchant ships;
She bringeth her food from afar"

CHAPTER 19

ESTHER SAW THE METCALFS regularly and soon became a member of the family. Esther was particularly close to Russell and called him "Uncle Metcalf," though just how she settled upon that moniker, no one could figure out.

She wrote long letters home to her parents, detailing her visits with the Metcalfs and how hospitable they had been. This greatly pleased Sofie, who began having strange nightmares after Esther had left for college. She attributed them to "empty nest syndrome" and having too much free time on her hands, but the content of her dreams was nonetheless disturbing. They always had Sofie back at Auschwitz, one or another of her dead stepdaughters holding their arms out to her in supplication. There had been the dream where poor Mirjam, wasted away from typhus, her body covered with sores, lay on the wooden bunk looking up at Sofie, asking why she wouldn't give her any medicine. Or the dream of Anneke screaming and clinging to Sofie as S. S. guards tried to drag her away to the gas chambers.

Then there was the one where Lena stood before her in their barrack, choking on the effects of Zyklon B and gasping for air, her eyes wide in surprise and panic, silently pleading for Sofie's help. The first time she had that dream, Sofie had begun screaming in her sleep. David had to shake her hard to wake her up. She was drenched in cold sweat and trembling. David had to hold her for a long while before she calmed down enough to go back to sleep.

But it was the dream about Jopie that occurred most often and upset her most. In this dream, Jopie stood alone in the middle of the train platform at the entrance to Auschwitz, dressed in her own clothes, her suitcase beside her. She seemed to be waiting for something or someone. But all she did was to ask, over and over, "Where is David? Why can't I find him?"

The night this dream first came to Sofie, she woke up and began to cry, softly so as not to wake David. It wasn't just the vision of her dead stepdaughter that saddened her; there was more to it than that. She wasn't sure what it was about that dream that made her feel so awful. Whatever this nagging feeling was, she didn't want to face it. Not yet. True to form, Sofie shook it off, determined not to let a silly dream make her imagination run amok.

Esther's four years at Jackson College went by with lightning speed. Before anyone knew it, it was time for her to graduate, and Sofie and David flew in from England to attend the ceremonies. The Metcalfs also planned to attend, and Sofie and Russell had a joyful reunion at Logan Airport, excited not only to see each other, but at long last to meet the spouses each had heard so much about.

Their spouses, however, were more than a little nervous about meeting the "significant other." David shook Russell's hand hesitantly, suddenly feeling very much out of place. Emily was more reserved than usual as she greeted Sofie, something that did not go unnoticed by Russell. After his many references to Emily's conviviality, Russell was embarrassed at this obvious change in her personality, certain that Soof would pick up on Emily's cool reception.

He needn't have worried, though. Sofie's delight in seeing her old friend and meeting his family eclipsed any awkwardness.

Graduation day dawned dry and sunny, the May air just warm enough to make for a perfect spring day. The Davidsons and the

Metcalfs sat together in the huge stadium, awaiting the procession of the graduates. Sofie permitted herself a little sigh of contentment. God had surely been good to her. She had been given a second chance at love and been blessed with a daughter she treasured, much as she had the six who were lost to her.

Sofie couldn't be more proud of Esther. Her daughter was an intelligent, warm-hearted, determined young woman who undoubtedly would make her mark on the world. Unfortunately, her outer beauty was marred by the facial disfigurement, but this imperfection had little impact on her positive self-image. Like Sofie's parents had done with her, Sofie made certain her own daughter grew up with the confidence that comes from unconditional love and acceptance. A healthy self-image can make any woman attractive, and though Esther didn't have many dates, Sofie was optimistic that one day some fine young man would take the time to look beyond the exterior and see the beautiful human being that was Esther.

A man like my Jan was, Sofie thought. If Esther's future husband is half the man Jan Rijnfeld was, she'll have all the happiness I could ever want for her ...

Her reverie was interrupted by the solemn strains of *Pomp and Circumstance*. The Jackson College Class of 1964 entered the stadium in pairs, marching in half-time to the music: right, together, left, together ... Families and friends seated in the many rows of folding chairs craned their necks to search for their graduate among the white caps and gowns. The graduates lined up alphabetically and it wasn't long before David spotted Esther.

"There she is!" he cried. Sofie and the Metcalfs stood up to get a better look, but only halfway, so as not to obstruct everyone else's view.

"I see her!" Emily Metcalf announced.

"Where?" Sofie demanded, frustrated that she couldn't spot her daughter as readily as everyone else seemed to.

Emily repositioned Sofie right in front of her and directed her eyes to where Esther stood. Finally, Sofie located her daughter. Everyone waved and Peter Metcalf put his two forefingers in his mouth and whistled shrilly.

"Peter!" Emily admonished.

David laughed. "Never mind, Emily, it worked!"

The piercing whistle had caught Esther's attention and she grinned happily at her little fan club. She raised her palm next to her body and waggled her fingers ever so slightly, unwilling to detract from her dignified posture.

The ceremonies commenced in earnest with droning speeches from various faculty members, the class valedictorian, and the keynote speaker. Finally the graduates filed up one by one to receive their diploma and handshakes from the dean. When at last it was Esther's turn, she was proud and poised as she accepted her diploma and the dean's congratulations. As she walked back to her seat, she switched her mortarboard tassel from the right side to the left, signifying that she was now graduated.

Sofie watched with tears of pride blurring her vision. She had traveled a long road to arrive at this moment. Looking at her daughter's happy smile as she cradled her diploma, Sofie knew that she would never forget this day.

As planned, Esther remained in the States to pursue graduate studies. When the Davidsons returned to England after graduation, Sofie exhibited all the signs of "empty nest syndrome." Even though Esther had been gone for the past four years, her absence at home struck Sofie anew, almost as if the college years were just a temporary absence. Now that Esther had graduated, Sofie felt a permanency in the vacant bedroom that stared back at her. She allowed herself one sentimental indulgence when she stood in the doorway of Esther's room and studied the childhood belongings left behind, reminiscing. After that, Sofie forbade herself to wallow in the loneliness felt by so many mothers whose mourning for grown children becomes an activity in itself.

" … as if the child was dead instead of just grown up," Sofie muttered.

She kept herself busy with volunteer work at the orphanage where they had adopted Esther. She and David traveled a good deal, even visiting Holland for the first time in many years, hopeful that family and friends had finally reconciled themselves to the Davidsons' marriage.

"If they haven't by now," Sofie declared, "They'll just have to get over it."

"Perhaps Mieneke and the boys have talked some sense into

them." David said, referring to Sofie's niece and nephews, now grown themselves.

Despite their daughter living so far away, Sofie and David felt at peace with their life. God had truly blessed them, for what he had taken away, he had returned twofold. Sofie never forgot the happiness she had with Jan and his six daughters, but she loved David and marveled at the second chance for love that had been given to her.

David was truly empathetic in Sofie's grief for the Rijnfeld family. Jopie had been his first love and she would always hold a special place in his heart, a place reserved for the kind of love you only feel the first time.

Sofie's life was full. She thought of her stepdaughters more often with laughter now than with sadness. She wished Esther could have known them. How they would have doted on her! In fact, Sofie mused, I really have the girls to thank for the blessings I enjoy now. I think I tried so hard to cultivate and strengthen their survival instinct, it must have strengthened me more than I realized.

If only she didn't dream of Jopie so often …

Sofie and David were experiencing a transition in their lives, but it was nothing compared to the changes that took place in the Metcalf family. Peter was drafted in 1966 and sent to Vietnam. Once again, Emily became consumed with worry over a loved one away at war. She was as alone in her fears now as she had been during World War II and Korea, for Russell was not the same easygoing, optimistic man she had married.

It wasn't just his lack of moral support that bothered Emily. Russell seemed so apathetic these days. He cared nothing about following the war's progress on television, and showed minimal interest in Peter's infrequent letters. It was as if Russell refused to acknowledge that Peter was even in Vietnam. Try as she might, Emily could not stimulate in him the response a father should have when his son's life is on the line.

So Emily fretted alone. The day the Marine lieutenant showed up at their front door accompanied by a Navy chaplain, Russell did not even cry with his wife when they received confirmation of Peter's death at

Khe San. Emily collapsed in Russell's arms at the news, and he held her and patted her woodenly. He thanked the chaplain and the lieutenant for their words of condolence, and helped Emily to the sofa where he sat with his arms around her, patting her all the while in a "there, there" gesture of comfort.

Not a tear did he shed.

Esther relayed the news to her parents, and Sofie immediately phoned Russell to say she wanted to fly in for the funeral. But Russell told her not to trouble herself. He appreciated her thoughtfulness, but it was a long, costly trip to make for such a sorrowful occasion. Besides, Emily hadn't been well lately and Russell needed to direct all his attention to her right now.

Sofie understood. She had never said as much to Russell, but she had always detected a hint of jealousy on Emily Metcalf's part. Often discernible to no one else, it is difficult for one woman to hide jealousy from another. She had often wondered if she should bring up the subject to Emily and reassure her that she had nothing to worry about. But what good would that do? If Emily was jealous over a friendship that was based more on letters than anything else; nothing Sofie could say would convince her otherwise. She felt badly about the misunderstanding, but some things were better left unsaid …

Sofie sent Esther and her new husband Barry Kaufman to the funeral as her emissaries. They would have attended, anyway; Esther was too fond of her Uncle Metcalf not to pay her respects to his family. She, too, had noticed a change in Russell over the past few years, a kind of sadness draped over him like gossamer. She mentioned it to her mother, but Sofie felt it best not to interfere, especially in light of Emily's insecurity where she was concerned.

Now that Esther was married and teaching library science at Emmanuel College in Boston, she saw less of the Metcalfs than she had during college. Twice a year, she and Barry visited her parents in England, bringing any tidbits of news that Russell may not have detailed to Sofie's satisfaction in his letters. Emily had recently been diagnosed with stomach cancer, and Sofie was more concerned than ever about Russell's state of mind. Would he be any more capable of facing his wife's illness than his son's death?

Esther reported that the last time she had seen the Metcalfs, Emily was very thin and perpetually tired, but holding her own. The prognosis, however, was not very good.

Time, in its inexorable way, moved on. Sofie's nightmares returned with alarming regularity. More and more frequently, it was Jopie who appeared in them to ask her stepmother where David was.

Sofie began to suspect that the dreams were a manifestation of suppressed guilt she felt for having married Jopie's fiancé. She explained her theory to David, but he didn't buy it.

"Soof, that's utter nonsense! You didn't steal me away from Jopie, you know.

"Didn't I? Maybe the real reason we married — the only reason — is because we grieved for the same person. That was our common ground. But we shouldn't have let it cloud our sensibilities."

"Our sensibilities? Soof, I love you for yourself, not because you're a link to Jopie. I thought you loved me for the same reason."

Sofie was silent. Perhaps she'd been dishonest with herself all along, and dishonest with David. She'd never had any romantic feelings toward him when Jopie was alive … was her marriage to him, after all, just an attempt to cling to a part of her life she couldn't let go of? The part that had been, really, the happiest?

David prodded her for an answer. "Well? Do you love me?"

The sad simplicity of her answer gave credence to her sincerity. "I love you, David. I just don't think I have the right to."

David was dumbfounded. She's really sold herself a bill of goods! She thinks she's committed some kind of immoral sin by marrying me.

Frustration and anger gave way to pain and dread as he recognized the inference of her declaration. A heavy chill settled in his chest.

Sofie knew her answer had hurt him and hated herself for it, but she knew it was the only answer she could give.

Sofie increasingly withdrew herself from her husband. She rebuffed his lovemaking overtures and moved into the guest room. During this period, the nightmares lessened in frequency, confirming Sofie's belief that she was not entitled to a life with David.

David begged Sofie to go with him to a marriage counselor, but she refused. Nothing a therapist had to say would change the way she felt inside. She was convinced that the only way to stop the dreadful nightmares altogether was to make things right.

"I've done Jopie a great injustice, David. We both have. But I should have known better."

David exercised considerable restraint in not exploding at this irrationality. "Sofie, I was not a little boy when we married. I was all grown up and making a decision I knew was right for me. I'm not the same man I was before the war. You're not the same woman. Can't you just accept the love that two people were lucky enough to find? Sofie and David are totally separate from Jopie and David."

It was the first time in years he had called her by her full name instead of the diminutive "Soof." David didn't want to appear angry, fearing it would only push her farther away. But he was supremely frustrated at the absurd conclusion she had drawn, and her stubborn refusal to seek professional help and try to save their marriage.

Anger and frustration dissipated into disbelief at Sofie's next words.

"I'm sorry, David. I know it's not fair to you this late in the game, but I owe it to Jopie. She didn't deserve to die like she did, and we took our happiness from her tragedy."

David sucked in his breath.

"We can't live our life on somebody else's demise. I'm sorry; I never meant to hurt you … I think we should get a divorce."

Esther and her husband moved to England with their baby son, fulfilling Esther's desire to be near her parents, now that they had split up. Esther was heartsick over the situation, but she of all people knew that once her mother made up her mind about something, there was nothing to be done.

Barry had lucked into a plum position that had become available with a London engineering firm, but would not remain vacant for long. It was grab it or lose it. Barry grabbed it.

Sofie was naturally delighted to have her children with her. For a while, she saw Esther several times a week: going to their flat for dinner, or having them all to dinner at her house. She really got to know her grandson and loved to get down on the floor to play with him. The baby chuckled gleefully at her antics, while Esther and Barry looked on, smiling.

One evening when they were gathered at Sofie's house, Barry took out an envelope from inside his jacket.

"I have something to show you, Soof. My father gave me these the other day." Barry opened the envelope and took out several wrinkled, stained photographs.

My great-aunt got these smuggled out of Westerbork during the war. I never knew her, but I thought perhaps you might recognize her. She was there around the same time you were.

Sofie examined the pictures. They looked to be family photos taken before the war. One was of a dignified-looking woman standing between two teenaged girls. Something about her was vaguely familiar.

"What was your great-aunt's name?" Sofie asked.

"How's this for a coincidence?" Barry said, turning to look at his wife. "Her name was Esther — Esther Lipkind."

Lipkind ... Lipkind ... no, Sofie didn't recognize the name. But the woman in the picture looked like someone she d seen before. Something about the stodgy face rang a bell ...

It couldn't be ... no, coincidences like this only happen in the movies. Was it possible that Barry's great-aunt was the same Esther for whom Sofie had named her own daughter?

She looked again at the photo and tried to convert the matronly image to the scraggly-haired, coarse creature who had first predicted their ultimate fate.

Yes, Sofie decided, it was possible. The concentration camps transformed people into unrecognizable entities that bore no resemblance to the civilized human beings snatched away from their lives by the Nazis.

Sofie had told her daughter about the woman she could never put out of her mind, and why she named her own child for her. Apparently, Esther Davidson Kaufman had made no connection between herself and her husband's great-aunt.

If this was the same woman, her legacy had been more than adequately preserved: she'd obviously had a family of her own, and a new great-niece who had been named after her. And if it wasn't the same

Esther, then Sofie was doubly gratified that she had given that poor soul she'd met in Westerbork a little piece of immortality.

Sofie decided not to bring up the question of this woman's identity to her children. What difference would it make? One thing was certain: life always comes full circle in its never-ending dance.

Gratified as she was at the direction her own life was taking, Esther cursed the timing of the move to England. After a year-long battle that took its toll on the entire family, Emily Metcalf succumbed to the cancer. She died with her husband and daughter at her bedside.

Susie Metcalf Warren bore her grief satisfactorily, thanks to the support of a kind husband and loving friends who sympathized with her double loss of brother and mother. Russell, however, was still in a strange world of his own. He acknowledged Emily's death and cried for her, something he hadn't been able to do for Peter. Susie saw this as a step in the right direction.

With Emily gone and Esther moving to England, Russell felt more depressed and alone than he had in his entire life. He told no one that Emily's dying words to him had been permission to marry Soof, now that he would be free and she was divorced from David ... Emily had always known Russell's feelings for Soof, but had thought she could compete ... she had lost him in the end, anyway ...

Russell had been adamant in his rebuttal. Emily must believe him ... yes, he cared for Soof, but not in the way Emily thought ... she was like a sister to him. No one could take the place of his Em ...

Despite his truthful denials, Emily Metcalf died believing that her husband really had been in love with Sofie Rijnfeld Davidson. But she harbored no bitterness toward either of them. If Sofie could make him happy where Emily had failed, then that's all she wanted for him.

Susie tried to convince her father to come to California and live with her family, but Russell knew that wouldn't work. Boston was his home, where he belonged. No, he would stay put.

In a perverse but positive way, Russell's newfound solitude was his salvation. After he said goodbye to Susie and her brood at Logan Airport, he drove home with an unheralded lightness of being. Something told him that it was time to return to life, such as it was, and finish living it. Always before, his retreat from reality was cushioned by Emily's grounding presence. Now he was on his own, and he thanked God he had awakened in time to save himself from becoming a doddering old man whose only company were the pigeons clamoring for the peanuts he threw to them in the Public Gardens.

Russell steered the car into the garage and shut the motor off. He sat there for a little while, postponing the inevitable moment when he must go into the all-too-empty house.

Okay, buddy boy, you can't sit in the car all night … get it over with.

He got out of the car and went inside the quiet house. It was the same as always, but Russell felt like he was really seeing it for the first time in years.

He went into the living room and sat in his favorite chair, the wing-back facing the mantle with its collection of family photographs. His eyes rested on one of Peter, smiling and proud in his Marine Corps uniform.

Okay, Dad, up and at 'em. You've got to take charge of your life now.

But it was the picture of Emily that spoke loudest to him.

Be like Sofie, Russ. Isn't her strength what you admired most about her?

Strength … that was for later. For right now, Russell bowed his head and cried.

"She opened her mouth with wisdom; And the law of kindness is on her tongue"

CHAPTER 20

The insistent jangle of the bedside telephone jolted Russell out of sleep. His heart was pounding and he felt disoriented. The phone rang again. Russell squinted at the face of the digital clock aglow in the darkness of the room. One-thirty. He picked up the phone, positive that something had happened to Susie or one of the grandchildren.

"Hello?"

A slight crackle, but no voice.

"Hello!" More insistently now.

The static grew louder, but this time Russell heard a female voice come through.

"Uncle Metcalf?"

Russell eased his breath out so Esther wouldn't hear his sigh of relief. It wasn't Susie or the grandkids, after all.

"Esther, dear, how nice to hear from you! Are you calling from London?"

"No, Uncle, I'm in Amsterdam. I'm sorry to wake you like this, but I had to call."

A pause.

Then, "Mum is dead."

Russell thought he must be dreaming. A sinking feeling in his gut grew heavier as Esther continued, confirming that it was no dream. He listened glumly as Esther explained that the whole family had traveled to Holland for a visit, and there Sofie had suffered a sudden heart attack. They had taken her by ambulance to a hospital. She stabilized, and for a while it looked as though everything would be all right. Then she had a second heart attack, the one that finished her.

" … and I knew you'd want to know." Esther's voice choked with emotion. "We're having her buried here in Holland. She had mentioned just the other day that she wanted to return home when she died, as she put it. We never dreamed … Perhaps she knew something we didn't."

"That would be just like your mother," Russell said. "She always tried to protect those she loved. When is the funeral, dear?"

"Not until Sunday. We have to wait until after the Sabbath."

Good. That gives me more time.

"Esther, would you mind if I flew out for the funeral? Or is it going to be just family?"

"Of course I don't mind, and yes, it is going to be just family," Esther replied without hesitation.

Russell warmed at the pointed inference to his inclusion as a family member.

"I'll be there tomorrow, dear. Hang in there. Let me speak to Barry for a minute."

Esther handed the phone to her husband and the two men made arrangements for Russell's arrival. If Russell would call with the flight information, Barry would make sure someone met him at the airport.

Russell said goodbye and put the phone back in its cradle. He was glad that dependable Barry was there. He would take care of the necessary details without burdening the family. He was someone Esther could lean on.

Not like me. I wasn't there for Emily …

No time for self-recriminations now. He rubbed the sleep from his face as the impact of Esther's news hit home. Within the past six years, Russell had lost both his son and his wife. Until now, he'd been unaware that he'd borne it all with the knowledge that he still had a special friend across the sea who shared a bond with him unlike any other. Someone who understood the depths of loss and how to overcome its devastating effects. Like so many others who had been a part of Sofie's life, Russell had absorbed some of the strength that emanated from her like rays of sunlight. Her courage bolstered them without their even realizing it.

Now the rays of light were forever dimmed and Russell was bereft. The knowledge that Sofie was somewhere in this world that had made him feel safe, able to endure. It mattered little that they spoke on the phone or saw each other only rarely; their connection was more perdurable than that.

Soof, teach me how to stand tall, as you always did.

As Russell got out of bed to pack for the trip to Amsterdam, he thought back to the war and their first meeting. He had been sent to Europe as a liberator. This time it was he who needed to be liberated from his emotional dependence on others. It was about time he learned to rely on his own fortitude.

Schiphol Airport continuously bustled with travelers from every corner of the world, as Amsterdam was a major gateway to many distant countries. Just outside customs, Esther stood fast against the tightly packed elbows and shoulders pushing against her as she waited for the arriving passengers to clear Immigration. Scanning the people coming through the double doors, she spotted Russell. Her hand shot in the air. "Uncle Metcalf!"

Russell waved back and steered his luggage cart toward her. He looks terrible, Esther thought. Thin and hollow-eyed. What's happened to him?

"Uncle Metcalf, it's so good to see you." Esther hugged him and felt the once-broad shoulders that now seemed fragile. She adjusted her glasses to look him over more thoroughly. "Are you all right?"

"Fine, dear, just fine," he said unconvincingly. "How are you holding up?"

"I suppose I'm all right. I mean, how good can I be at a time like this? I'm just happy you've come. It means a lot to me. It would have meant a lot to Mum."

Russell regarded Esther's calm demeanor and erect posture, and acknowledged Sofie's success in infusing her daughter with her own strong character.

Valuable traits to have in this day and age, he thought. They will serve Esther well in life.

"Mum's body is being prepared for the burial tomorrow," Esther went on. "We were able to find a local *chevra kadisha* to perform the rite of washing the body."

"Will there be a viewing?" Russell asked. He would like to see Soof's face one last time.

"No, Uncle, open caskets are forbidden in Judaism."

Esther linked her arm through Russell's as she steered him toward the exit. "Anyway, it's better if we remember Mum the way we knew her best: laughing and cheerful, meeting every new challenge with a vengeance."

God, Esther was eulogizing her already! Russell winced. But she was right, of course. Russell conjured that very image of Soof every time he read one of her letters, or listened to one of Esther's family anecdotes. Very often, that image was followed by another: Soof sitting on an upturned crate in the displaced persons camp, relating to Russell the story of her internment at Auschwitz.

The two visualizations always buoyed his morale. Whenever he felt overwhelmed, he thought of Sofie. It brought back some of the fighting spirit he had lost. He vowed he would not lose it again. Come hell or high water, he was going to be like his friend Soof and deal with the realities of life, good or bad. Let that be his tribute to her.

If only he'd come to his senses before Emily had died … no, don't dwell on the "if onlys." He'd made his mind up to look to the future and not to the past. He'd made mistakes that could never be rectified, but he still had a daughter left who deserved the kind of father he once was and determined to be again. He'd be a doting grandfather too.

The hour of solitude had passed. Time now to reach out.

The laws of Judaism which govern the ways of death and mourning are precise, carried out with the utmost respect for the deceased. The ritual of *tahara* — the cleansing of the dead — is no exception. Combined with the duty of the *shomer* — the guardian who remains with the body until burial, offering continuous prayer — this holy rite ensures that the deceased is never alone. Just as a newborn child is immediately washed, entering the world clean and pure, so must the departed be cleansed and purified when they leave this world. Modesty is maintained at all times, with women attending to women and men attending to men.

It is considered a *mitzvah* to perform this service, and volunteer teams of lay persons in the Jewish community comprise the *chevra kadisha,* the "holy society."

Sofie's niece, Mieneke, couldn't think of a more fitting way to bid a final goodbye to her beloved aunt than to participate in her *tahara.* As children, Mieneke and her brothers had adored their Tante Soof and had always wished she would visit more often from England. Mieneke now lived in the States, but immediately flew to Amsterdam when her cousin Esther called to tell her of Tante's death.

There was no idle conversation among Mieneke and the other members of the *chevra kadisha.* The solemnity of the ritual must not be disturbed. Sofie was accorded the same respect as if she were alive. Before they commenced the washing, Mieneke offered up the traditional prayer:

> *O God of kindness and mercy, whose ways are*
> *merciful and truthful, Thou hast commanded us*
> *to practice righteousness and truth with the dead*
> *and engage in properly burying them … May it*
> *therefore be Thy will, O Lord our God, to give*
> *us fortitude and strength to properly perform*
> *our undertaking of this holy task of cleaning*
> *and washing the body, and putting on the*
> *shroud, and burying the deceased …*

As one of the women continued reciting prayers, Mieneke and the others began the actual washing. Approximately 24 quarts of water divided into 3 vessels were used to cleanse each section of the body, with the vessels rotated in sequence so that water is continuously poured. With one hand, Mieneke lifted the right side of the white sheet covering Tante Soof's supine body. In the other hand, she held a ewer with eight quarts of water.

Mieneke lightly covered Sofie's mouth with her hand to prevent any water from entering. Beginning at the head, she slowly and reverently poured water from the pitcher down the right side of Sofie's body. Just before her vessel was emptied, the next woman began pouring from hers.

Mieneke checked to make sure that none of Tante Soof's fingers were clenched, which might prevent water from reaching all skin surfaces. She observed Soof's hands, bare of her favorite ruby-red nail polish in accordance with the ritual. Soof's lips, too, were without the bright lipstick Mieneke fondly remembered in conjured images of her aunt's smiling face.

As the third vessel was emptied onto the lower portion of Sofie's right side, the bearer intoned:

> *And I will pour upon you pure water,*
> *and ye shall be cleansed; from all your*
> *uncleanliness and abomination will I*
> *purify you.*

The women replaced the sheet over the body and uncovered Sofie's left side for a repetition of the process. Mieneke watched the stream of water cascade down Tante Soof's left arm. She caught sight of the small red scar on the inside of her forearm. It was the scar that had raised so many questions during Mieneke's childhood. She touched it softly. It felt smoother than she remembered. How well she recalled Tante Soof's stories of Auschwitz and Westerbork, of hunger and deprivation, things her own parents refused to talk about. Mieneke smiled to herself at Tante's typical head-on approach to life. Secrets are unhealthy, she used to say. Once you know the truth, you can face anything.

The cleansing completed on the front side, the ritual must be repeated on the back. It was forbidden to denigrate the deceased by placing her face-down on the wooden cleansing board, so the washing must be done with the body resting on its side. Together, the *chevra kadisha* turned Sofie's body on its right side. Continuously pouring the water, they cleansed the back, again starting at the head and working downward towards the feet. After they carefully dried the body, she was again lowered onto her back. With no small effort, the women turned Sofie's bulk onto the left side and repeated the ritual.

Finally, Mieneke took up a small knife and carefully cracked open an egg near the narrow end, removing only the top piece of shell. She poured a few drops of wine into the egg within the shell and stirred it. In keeping with time-honored custom, she then brushed some of the egg-wine mixture across Sofie's forehead. This symbolized the cyclical nature of life. As the shape of the egg is without end, so is the wheel of life, forever turning in an endless circle.

Once the entire body was washed and dried and Sofie's hair combed neatly into place, the *chevra kadisha* dressed the body in the prescribed shroud. The ensemble consisted of white linen trousers, shirt, and an overgarment that included a girdle or belt. Sometimes more pieces were included in the set, but never fewer than the three in which they clad Tante Soof. The garments were without pockets, since no material goods are taken by the deceased into the next world. There were no knots or seams in the garments. Mieneke was glad that they were not using the *mitznephet*, the headdress sometimes placed over the departed's entire head. She didn't think she could stand to see Tante Soof's head covered like an Egyptian mummy.

The trousers were donned easily and tied at the waist with a drawstring. Its ends were loosely arranged to form the Hebrew letter *shin*, the first letter in the Hebrew word for God. Putting on the shirt was a little trickier, requiring two of the women raising the upper torso while Mieneke and another drew the arms into the sleeves and slipped the garment over the head. Lastly, the *kittel*, or overgarment, was drawn over the body, the arms placed in its sleeves. It was tied loosely at the neck in the same manner as the shirt and trousers, the strings forming the shape of the *shin*.

The ritual was nearly complete. Mieneke smoothed a few locks of Tante Soof's wavy hair that had been mussed in the dressing process, and studied the woman on the slab. She half expected to be frightened by the picture Tante Soof now presented, but all she saw was her aunt, albeit strangely garbed. The face was slack, but it wore a look of peace. The skin was plump and smooth, flawless as a baby's. The cheek still felt soft to Mieneke's touch.

Mieneke looked up to see the other three women standing by in silence, waiting patiently while Mieneke spent these last private moments with her aunt. But the time had come to place the body in the casket, and it would take all four of them to lift Sofie's ample body from the slab.

Mieneke realized that it was this part of the ritual she had subconsciously been dreading. It seemed so — final.

With as much dignity and respect as they could maintain, the *chevra kadisha* lifted the stout body from the slab and placed it gently into the plain pine casket. Three holes had already been drilled in the bottom of the coffin to expedite decomposition and fulfill the Biblical dictum, " … dust thou art, and unto dust shalt thou return."

A linen bag containing some straw and a handful of earth from Israel had already been placed in the coffin. The women straightened Sofie's garments, slightly out of breath from their exertion. Again, they stood silent, waiting for Mieneke to give them a signal.

For the last time, she looked upon her aunt. She pressed a light kiss to her forehead. "Goodbye, Tante Soof. I'll miss you."

Tears pooled in her eyes and she fumbled in her pocket for a handkerchief. She dabbed at the corners of her eyes and nodded her assent to the other women, who carried out the final duty of the *chevra kadisha* and asked forgiveness of the deceased.

With that, the coffin lid was closed.

"She riseth also while it is yet night,

And giveth food to her household,

And a portion to her maidens."

CHAPTER 21

" ... *EL MALAY RACHAMIM, SHOCHANE
bahm'romim* ... O God, full of compassion, Thou who dwellest on high,
grant perfect rest beneath the sheltering wings of Thy presence, among
the holy and pure who shine as the brightness on the heavens, unto the
soul of Sofie Davidson, who has gone unto eternity ... "

The cantor concluded the haunting melody of the memorial
prayer, so different from the Mourner's *Kaddish*. Mieneke was moved by
the *El malay rachamim*; she particularly liked the invocation " ... may the
Lord of Mercy bring her under the cover of His wings forever ... "

Tante Soof has earned her rest, Mieneke thought. She spent
almost her whole life looking out for others; now it was her turn to be
protected.

There were sniffles and an occasional nose blown loudly into
a handkerchief. The rabbi began the eulogy he'd prepared after
interviewing Esther and some of Sofie's other relatives.

"I've often been asked by the children in my congregation, 'Where
was God during the Holocaust?' Indeed, where do we find God's
presence in a tragedy such as the Holocaust?

Perhaps He showed Himself in the many individual acts of

kindness, selflessness, martyrdom, and rebellion which took place throughout Nazi-occupied Europe.

The woman to whom we say goodbye today was a shining example of God's presence manifested in her deeds …"

Mieneke considered the rabbi's words. She hadn't thought about it that way before, but what the rabbi said was true. God had been present at Auschwitz, despite evidence to the contrary. And at Buchenwald and Belsen and Majdanek and Dachau …

Perhaps this had been Tante Soof's purpose in life: to reach out and succor those who were not blessed with much strength of their own.

Mieneke recollected the stories she had heard of Tante Soof's six stepdaughters. She tried to imagine herself in their situation: a teenager sent off to an arcane fate by a tyrannical dictator who hated you not for who you were but for what you were. How terrified they must have been! For the first time, Mieneke felt she fully understood the magnitude of Tante Soof's decision to stay with her stepdaughters through whatever the Nazis had in store for them.

Mieneke closed her eyes and visualized Tante Soof's face. This time she saw, behind the laughing hazel eyes, a patina of pain deeply felt. You had to look hard to detect even a glimmer of it, for Sofie had become expert in hiding it, masking the pain with hope and gladness. She had refused to allow the ghosts of Auschwitz to haunt her. Mieneke could hear her aunt now, defiant and determined.

I have survived. What matters is the future. What good does it do to dwell on past pain? To do so forestalls healing.

Even now, Mieneke felt a respectful awe for Tante Soof's amazing outlook on life. To have lived in hell and still greet the day with a welcoming smile was an achievement far greater than any Mieneke had ever known. When she once told her aunt as much, Sofie had merely replied, "I smile because I wake each morning to find that heaven is right here on earth, as surely as hell had been."

Mieneke brought herself out of her own thoughts in time to hear the rabbi's conclusion of the eulogy. It was from the Talmud:

Whoever saves a single life is as one who saved an entire world.

196

Jewish law mandates that the casket must be lowered in the presence of the mourners. Not only is it considered an aspersion to the deceased to turn one's back upon an unburied casket, but to witness the actual burial reaffirms to the mourners that the death of their loved one is indeed a reality.

Mieneke stood soberly by as the coffin was lowered into the grave. She deferred to her cousin Esther's family as they observed one more ritual. Each took a shovelful of earth and dropped it on top of the casket. David Davidson, although divorced from Tante Soof, grieved no less than the others and he, too, participated in this. The family all knew why Sofie had divorced David, but they also knew that David had never stopped loving her. Everyone still considered him part of the family, which comforted David enormously. The divorce had hurt him badly, and the family's support was a balm, especially in light of their early disapproval of Sofie and David's marriage.

When he was finished, David placed the shovel on the ground according to custom, instead of passing it directly to the next person. Mieneke retrieved it, shoveled a small amount of earth, and let it fall onto the casket. Dust unto dust …

She lay the shovel down again. Then she saw Esther nod to a strange man whom Mieneke had never seen before, encouraging him to pick up the shovel and participate in the ritual. The man hesitantly picked up the shovel and did as he had seen Esther and the others do. Mieneke noted that he seemed comfortable around Esther and her family, yet he did not join in the Hebrew repetition of the Mourner's *Kaddish*.

The rabbi offered his final prayer. "May the Lord comfort you among the other mourners of Zion and Jerusalem" — and the service was over.

Now the mourners greeted one another, shaking hands, offering condolences, sharing hugs. After speaking with Esther and Barry, Mieneke's eyes sought out the strange man. He was standing alone near the gravesite, hands deep in his trenchcoat pockets.

Mieneke gave Esther's hand a final squeeze and moved toward him.

"Excuse me, I don't believe we've met. I'm Mieneke Gold, Sofie's niece."

The man's face lit up at this pleasant surprise. "From Israel! Soof has told me all about you."

Mieneke smiled at the familiar nickname. "Actually, I live in the States now. My husband is from Tennessee."

Russell nodded, then they fell silent. Mieneke looked at him expectantly.

"I'm sorry, you are … ?"

"Forgive me — my name is Russell Metcalf. I met your aunt in Europe when I was in the army. She had just been liberated from Auschwitz."

They shook hands. A spark of recollection flickered in Mieneke's brain. This must be Tante Soof's American soldier friend her mother had once told her about. Apparently he and Tante Soof had kept in touch all these years.

Russell's face suddenly contorted. "Are you all right, Mr. Metcalf?" Mieneke asked in concern.

Russell wiped his eyes with his handkerchief. "I'm sorry, Mieneke. I lost my wife and son a few years ago, and now with Soof gone — " His voice trailed off.

Mieneke laid a comforting hand on his arm. She didn't realize Tante Soof and Mr. Metcalf had been that close. But then, she'd lived in Israel for several years and then the States, so she wasn't too up on family gossip.

She took in Russell's sad face. "You're coming back to my parents' home, aren't you? Please, you must."

"No, my dear, thank you. I shouldn't intrude on a family gathering."

"Mr. Metcalf, you wouldn't be here if Tante Soof hadn't considered you part of the family. Come, let me drive you."

Russell acquiesced to Mieneke's cajoling. "I'll go on one condition: that you call me Russell."

Mieneke smiled. "It's a deal."

He allowed her to lead him away. In fact, he was glad. He wanted to prolong this pleasant feeling of acceptance that being with Soof's family evoked.

As they walked toward the blue Saab parked nearby, Mieneke noted that some of the sadness on Russell's face had dissipated. She was glad she had convinced him to come home with her.

During the short drive to Mieneke's parents' home, Russell entertained her with the story of his first meeting with Soof and the lifelong friendship that ensued. Mieneke marveled at the way fate can bring people together, and was impressed with the power of Tante Soof's never-say-die motto which so obviously had affected Russell Metcalf. How many other people's lives had she influenced in that way?

Back at the house, mourners gathered to take comfort in one another's company and to partake of the eggs, olives, and other round foods that again symbolized the unending cycle of life. The family greeted Russell warmly, reassuring him that not only was he welcome there, he belonged there. All were touched by his obvious esteem for Sofie.

It had been a long, emotionally draining day, and toward the late afternoon everyone was tired. Russell dreaded returning to his lonely hotel room, but he didn't want to overstay his welcome with Sofie's family. Anyway, he needed to start packing and reconfirm his return flight reservation ...

Mieneke protested that he didn't need to leave yet but he insisted, so she agreed to drive him back to his hotel. It was a quiet ride, both immersed in their own thoughts. The front windows were rolled down and Russell breathed deeply of the damp evening air. Mieneke pulled the Saab up to the curb in front of the hotel entrance. Russell thanked her for all she had done and said how wonderful it had been to meet her.

"Are you going to be all right?" Mieneke questioned. "I don't like to think of you making such a long trip home alone." Her concern was genuine, but she worried how patronizing she must sound.

"I'll be fine, dear." Russell got out of the car and pushed the door shut with his hands over the juncture of the doorframe and lowered window.

He stuck his head inside. "You know, I think I finally pinned down what the problem is."

"Problem?"

"Something that's been bothering me all day. I couldn't put my finger on it until tonight." Russell gave Mieneke a rueful smile. "The loss I feel is not so much from Sofie's death itself. We all have to die sometime, and she lived a fuller life than most people … Of course, I'll miss her …"

Mieneke was tired and grew a tad impatient at his rambling. She wished he would get to the point.

" … but much as I'll miss Soof, the real tragedy is that now her story is over."

Mieneke frowned. "I'm not sure I follow you."

"When Sofie was alive, she made a difference in people's lives just by her very presence. That's a marvelous gift that few are privileged to enjoy. Now that she's gone, no one else will ever receive that gift.

Mieneke digested this unexpected revelation. To her, Tante Soof had always been her fun-loving aunt. She hadn't thought of her in terms of the ministering angel about whom Russell waxed lyrical. How marvelous to have someone who's not even a blood relative feel so deeply about … well, about who you are. She wondered if Tante Soof had realized the high regard this man had for her.

Mieneke felt as though she didn't know her aunt as well as she thought she had. This man was introducing her to a woman she'd never seen. Too late she was learning how much more there was to the robust woman who had always been just cheerful, plump Tante Soof. If only there had been more time …

All this flashed through Mieneke's mind in an instant. Not knowing what else to say to Russell, she answered, "I see."

"I just wish everyone knew what a special woman Sofie was," Russell sighed. "She's lived through so much that would have broken a lesser person."

A glow of understanding welled up inside Mieneke, coupled with a desire to eliminate the pathos etched on Russell's face.

She reached over from the driver's seat and covered his age-spotted hand with her own. "Don't worry, Russell. I promise you Tante Soof won't be forgotten. I'm going to make certain of it."

Russell smiled indulgently, doubting if Mieneke really understood what he'd been trying to say. He gave her hand a final pat and turned into the hotel.

Mieneke watched him walk away. This strange, sad old man had appeared out of nowhere to declare the importance of Tante Soof in his life. How odd. And how wonderful. She sat in the car for many minutes after Russell was out of sight, contemplating what he had said.

Russell had a point. Tante Soof's story should not end here just because her life is over. People should know what an extraordinary woman she was. And if Mieneke had anything to say in the matter, Tante Soof would live forever.

EPILOGUE

I made a promise, that long ago night, to myself as well as to Russell Metcalf, that Tante Soof would indeed live on. People would know that a woman named Sofie Mecklenberg Rijnfeld Davidson had made a difference in this world. They would also know how strong is the will to survive, and the unendurable horrors that become endurable when life is the prize.

I realized too that by sharing Tante Soof's story, other survivors might be encouraged to share their own experiences. No children should grow up bewildered by unanswered questions, as I was. Understanding can only emerge from communication. Tante Soof knew that. She explained to me what my parents could not. Now she would tell the world.

Tante Soof was special. Not only because she was my aunt, but because she possessed the kind of human spirit that refuses to be beaten. Hers is but one of countless stories of courage and tenacity, and in each there is a lesson to be learned. Certainly, she was fallible — what human being isn't? But without the imperfections that are interwoven into one's character, there can be no personal triumph. Tante Soof reminds me of the mythological phoenix that rises undaunted from the ashes, unable to be destroyed. She touched so many lives. She made the world a more colorful place.

"A woman of valor
who can find?
For her price
is far above rubies."